thinking about grades . . .

Blake: "I don't understand girls. Like Rainey. I thought we had an *understanding,* and then she goes and practically marries Tucker while I'm away. I just don't get it. And I sure don't like it."

Rainey: "Falling for Tucker just sort of happened . . . he's fun, and Blake wasn't even around. But since C.G. told me Tucker's been putting the moves on other girls, I'm confused. Who needs love, anyway?"

Michael: "I never met anyone like C.G. before. The fire! The passion! The way she fixed my carburetor! People say she's bad news, but maybe they just don't know her like I do. She's okay . . . I hope."

Ann Lee: "I thought when I got back from Europe everyone would see I'm different. Smarter, more sophisticated—cosmopolitan, even. But no one seems to have noticed. Least of all Michael. I'll have to do something about that."

Susan: "I always thought being in love with Jesse would be enough . . . and it's wonderful, it really is. But this year everything is so different. Sometimes I even think I might not make homecoming queen. But that's crazy . . . isn't it?"

Books by Janice Harrell

EASY ANSWERS
SENIOR YEAR AT LAST
WILD TIMES AT WEST MOUNT HIGH

Available from ARCHWAY Paperbacks

SENIOR YEAR
at Last

Janice Harrell

AN ARCHWAY PAPERBACK
Published by POCKET BOOKS
New York   London   Toronto   Sydney   Tokyo   Singapore

AN ARCHWAY PAPERBACK *Original*

An Archway Paperback published by
POCKET BOOKS, a division of Simon & Schuster Inc.
1230 Avenue of the Americas, New York, NY 10020

ISBN: 0-671-68572-4

First Archway Paperback printing May 1990

10 9 8 7 6 5 4 3 2 1

AN ARCHWAY PAPERBACK and colophon are
registered trademarks of Simon & Schuster Inc.

Printed in the U.S.A.

IL 6+

ONE

C. G. Bowman's short black hair was combed behind her ears, boy-style. Her black eyes smoldered in a way that always made people check behind themselves for some oncoming natural disaster, like a tornado. What they soon realized was that it was C.G. herself who was the disaster.

She had never been a good citizen. In the ninth grade her science fair project was a whiskey still. Revenue agents came into the school and broke up her display with hatchets, adding a lot of excitement to that year's fair.

C.G. washed behind her ears only when she felt like it; she bit her nails to the quick; and she smoked like a chimney. The gold studs in her earlobes, which looked as if they'd been set in with a rivet gun, neatly matched the studs on her leather jacket. All the other girls at West Mount High were afraid of her.

On the whole, it was good for Susan Brantley's peace of mind that she hadn't noticed C.G. mounting her motorcycle near the picnic tables beyond the tennis courts in the park.

"Blake!" Susan called.

A lean boy put his tennis racket in the back of his red Corvette. In the waning light of the summer evening, his tennis whites shone luminous against his tanned legs. "Hey, Susan. What's going on?"

"You're home! Everybody's coming back to town! It's great. You wouldn't believe how dead it's been this summer. I'm actually looking forward to school starting. I'm serious."

Suddenly a sound like that of a chain saw rent the air, and a motorcycle cut close between the two, leaving a cloud of dust in its wake. Susan spluttered and tried to wave away the haze of grit. To her surprise Blake was grinning.

"What's so funny?"

"That was C.G. I didn't know she was back in town."

"Aw, gee," Susan gasped. "I sort of hoped she was dead." When Susan had said how great it was that people were coming back to town, she had most emphatically not meant C.G. Susan still remembered the day two years before, when C.G. knocked Missy Melinik into the mall fountain and broke her arm. Equally memorable was the night Mr. Anders's utility shed was blown up. There was no proof that C.G. was responsible for the explosion, but she had been seen in the library reading a book called *Terrorism: A Handbook.* After those two incidents Missy Melinik had begged her parents to let her go away to boarding school.

"I heard C.G. went to live with her father," said Blake.

"I guess he couldn't handle her, either, so he sent her back."

The park lights suddenly went on overhead, turning Susan's crimped blond hair into a halo around her heart-shaped face. She watched as the motorcycle paused at the park entrance and noticed that in a rare exercise of prudence, C.G. had strapped on her helmet. After checking the traffic with a quick glance each way, she roared away.

Susan made a face. "That's one person I don't have to worry about inviting to my party, anyway."

"What party?"

"My back-to-school party." She pulled an index card out of her pocket and looked at it with satisfaction.

Blake took the card from her. " 'Paper streamers, pig cooker, Ann Lee, staple gun, Michael'?"

She snatched it back. "I'm just getting organized."

"Looks like you've got a long way to go."

"Watch it. You'd better be nice to me or I won't invite you. It's going to be a *huge* bash. I didn't think my mother would ever say I could have it, but suddenly—just like that—she gave in!"

"I don't see Rainey's name on the list."

Susan stuck the card back in her pocket. "I figured Rainey would probably be working that night. Anyway, the party's just in the planning stages." The truth was Susan hadn't decided whether she was going to invite Rainey or not. This was the sort of thing she would have liked to hash over at delicious length with her best friend, but Ann Lee had gone to Belgium on a summer exchange program instead of staying and helping out when she was needed. It was typical of the unfairness of life, Susan thought, that C. G. Bowman was back in town and Ann Lee was not.

Blake stood so still he was beginning to make Susan nervous. "Look," he said suddenly, "you remember how you owe me a favor? I want you to ask Rainey to the party and I don't want you to ask Tucker."

"I can't do that! Tucker lives only a couple of blocks away, and his parents see my parents all the time. It would look weird."

"You owe me one, remember?"

"What if Rainey asks if she can bring Tucker? I've seen them together an awful lot this summer."

Blake looked away so she could not see his face. "Tell her nobody's bringing a date."

"But that would be a lie."

"You've never told a lie?" His brown eyes met hers, and it was Susan's turn to feel uncomfortable. Generally she was an honest person, but it was true that during an awkward period when she had had to sneak around to date Jesse McCracken, Blake had helped cover for her with her parents. And it was also true that she had promised to pay him back for the favor. But that was way back in February or March. If he had had a shred of human decency he would have forgotten all about it by now.

Still, she supposed she should count herself lucky that it wasn't anything worse. Blake hadn't asked her to do anything totally embarrassing. She could simply tell Tucker his invitation had gotten lost in the mail, she decided. "Okay," she said. "I'll see what I can do."

"Strike!" the umpire yelled. On the baseball diamond, the uniformed players were changing positions.

"Oh, my gosh!" Susan cried. "This is it! The last inning. It's up to Jesse to strike them out now."

Blake glanced in at the diamond. "I've never figured out why people get excited about baseball. It's so slow. Half the time nobody out there's doing anything."

"I've got to go," Susan said abruptly. " 'Bye." She hurried back to take her seat on the bleachers. She became so intent on the game that she didn't notice when Blake's Corvette drove away. It wasn't that she was a big baseball fan but rather that she felt she had to give Jesse moral support. Baseball was the focus of his life. It was why he played with the city league during the summer when most high school ball players were taking a break. He was the star of the West Mount High team, and he had realistic hopes of going pro. With his cool head and his 85 mph fast ball, he seemed to have been designed by God for pitching. Unfortunately, that evening he was not in top form.

Susan bit her lip and watched him anxiously. A summer spent working on his uncle's farm had bleached Jesse's hair until it looked almost white under the lights. He glanced away from the batter, then quickly looked forward and released the ball. It was a pale blur flying over the plate. "Stri-ike!" called the umpire as it smacked into the catcher's glove.

"Way to go!" yelled the man sitting behind Susan.

Susan heard a mosquito and reflexively slapped at her ankle.

On the pitcher's mound Jesse paused for a minute, breathing steadily. Suddenly he looked up, drew his arm back, and sent the ball over the plate like a shot.

The umpire called a ball.

"Rotten call, you idiot!" someone bellowed behind her.

5

The fat man next to Susan bit into a marshmallow-and-chocolate pie and dropped the cellophane wrapper under the bleachers.

Susan frowned. She knew it was tough for Jesse to play ball after a full day's work mowing and stacking hay. She could see fatigue in the slope of his shoulders. Sure enough, his next pitch was wild, and the batter had to jump back. The pitch after that knocked over the water jug by the players' bench.

Jesse wiped his face with his sleeve and stared at the dark woodlands that rimmed the north side of the park. Susan held her breath. She knew he was trying to recover his concentration. Just then he pulled back and sent another ball sailing across the plate. "Stri-ike!"

What followed was painful for Susan to watch. Perfect pitches alternated with throws that were pure slapstick. Susan wished she could go out and gather Jesse up in her arms the way a mother might gather up a tired child for a nap. But she couldn't. She had to sit there as Jesse slowly pitched his way to a loss.

The game was finally over. The players slapped one another wearily on the back and slumped off to their cars. Susan climbed down from the bleachers and walked out to Jesse, who was still standing on the mound staring down at the dirt. His jaw was clenched.

She put her arm around him, feeling the dampness where the sweat had soaked into his shirt. "There'll be other games."

"Stop it." His voice was tight. "Don't try to comfort me, okay?"

She didn't say anything else. They walked together out

to the parking area. Jesse thrust his hands into his pockets. "Who was that nut on the motorcycle?" he said in a constricted voice. She could tell he was trying to snap out of his mood. "Bill Taylor nearly dropped the bat when that thing came through. You'd think people would have more sense."

"That was C. G. Bowman."

"Jeez, I thought she was in jail or something."

"We should be so lucky."

What made C.G. a special problem for Susan was that C.G.'s mother had once been in Susan's mother's bridge club. Every now and then Mrs. Brantley would say, "I want you to be nice to C.G., Susan. She still hasn't adjusted to her parents' divorce." But Susan had no intention of going near C.G., much less being nice to her. She didn't want to end up like Missy Melinik—swimming in the fountain at the mall.

When they got into his car, Jesse sat behind the wheel a minute and stared sightlessly into space. "I was doing okay until that last inning. Then—I don't know, I just fell apart."

Susan knew that he was going to have to go over every play, every error, every single component of the downhill slide of that last inning. It was awful to have something matter so much to you, she thought, stifling a sigh. "Let's go get something to eat," she said.

By the time they got out of the car at the Burger King, Susan had heard all about the shortcomings of the catcher and the inattentiveness of the umpires and the weaknesses of the batters. The phrase *play-by-play account* took on new meaning when Jesse started dissecting a ball game. He was as concerned with each minute detail as a heart surgeon

7

repairing damaged arteries. But Susan had no impulse to smile. She heard the hurt pride behind his words and only wished she could do something to help.

"I don't know," Jesse said gloomily. "Maybe I just can't cut it. Who am I kidding? I'm the one that blew it."

Susan recognized this as the inevitable finale to the discussion of any losing game. Each time the conclusion that he was a pitcher of no talent struck him with the force of revelation. He never remembered that he had come to the same startling conclusion the last time his team lost.

She held his hand and pushed open the door of the restaurant. "You're tired. You're going to feel better tomorrow."

"I hope." Jesse shivered when they stepped from the warm night into the air conditioning. "Was that Blake I saw talking to you? Is he back?"

"Everybody's coming back." In spite of her concern about Jesse, Susan felt a pleasant flutter of excitement when she thought of her party. "I'm really glad. It's been so dead around here."

"Am I supposed to take that personally?"

"No, stupid." She punched him lightly. She hoped junk food calories would improve his morale. It wouldn't hurt, either, she figured, to get his mind off baseball for a while.

A couple of minutes later they found a place to sit and unwrapped their burgers. Susan took a bite of hers, her eyes checking Jesse's face. At least his jaw was no longer clenched. That was a good sign. She lifted a sheaf of papers out of her straw bag and laid them on the table. "Take a look at these."

"What's this?"

"I want to see what you think about them. These are Ann Lee's letters."

"You mean she wrote all those letters in just one summer?" Jesse eyed the letters mistrustfully. "Thick enough, aren't they?"

"But they get thinner. See?" Susan spread them out before him in chronological order. "They start out being seven pages long and they sound just like Ann Lee. Like, they're full of descriptions of museums and how she's all excited thinking about her wonderful cultural opportunities and how she's worried about the responsibility of being an ambassador of goodwill for the United States and all that stuff."

"She could stand to lighten up a little."

"She has." Susan picked up her friend's most recent letter and frowned at it. "One page! Just one page! All it says is, 'Having terrific time. See you soon. Love to the guys. *Ciao.*' "

"Chow?"

"It's Italian for hello. Also goodbye."

"I thought she went to Belgium."

"The *important* thing is that the letters just get shorter and shorter and somewhere or other she quit talking about museums. She hasn't said one word about cultural opportunities since the Fourth of July! What can it mean?"

"I don't see what you're getting at. Anybody would get tired of museums. That's just normal."

"This is Ann Lee, the girl who won the citizenship prize three years running! This is the girl who tells her blind dates about the national debt!"

"What's getting to you, Susan?"

"I don't know," she said slowly. "I guess I have this

fear she's going to show up all cosmopolitan and be—different.''

He grinned. ''Instead of being like you—dull and stay-at-home?''

She kicked him under the table. ''Don't be ridiculous.'' Though Susan didn't like to admit it, Jesse had put his finger on what was really bothering her. It had always been Susan who glittered, Susan who took the lead in the class play, Susan who attracted the boys. She had been the star of the show while Ann Lee had been cast firmly in a supporting role. For years Susan had been urging Ann Lee to come out of herself more, to wear more exciting clothes, to talk to boys. What if she had at last? Susan wanted her dependable ally back. She didn't want to be faced with some European sophisticate.

''You think I'm being silly, don't you?''

''I didn't say that,'' he said.

''That's what you were thinking, though.''

''Well, look at yourself. You're all set to freak out just because Ann Lee's letters have gotten short.''

''That's not the only thing. It's the *tone* of them. It's what's been left out. But you think I'm worrying about nothing, don't you?''

''You said it. I didn't.''

''I guess you're right. I know it's great that we're going to be seniors and everything.'' Susan shifted uncomfortably. ''But I guess one part of me doesn't want anything to change.''

He took her hand. ''Hey, get a grip. It's going to be okay.''

She smiled weakly. It was funny to hear him telling her to cheer up when he was practically suicidal over losing a stupid ball game. Hearing a roaring noise, Susan glanced outside. A small figure on a motorcycle had pulled up at the traffic light. It was C. G. Bowman. Susan couldn't help but feel that was a bad omen.

Two

"**S**usan? Michael here. Just got your invitation and I'll be ready to party!"

Susan held the receiver away from her ear. When Michael Dessaseaux was enthusiastic he was also loud. "Great. So you can make it, then?"

"You bet. The only reason I'm calling is I want to know if it's okay if I bring a girl."

"Sure—I guess." Susan felt a slight qualm as she remembered telling Rainey no one was bringing a date, but she quashed it.

"When's Ann Lee getting back?" Michael asked.

"She flew in this morning. I was going to go over and see her, but her mom says she's still sleeping. Jet lag, I guess. She'll be at the party, though."

"I just hope she doesn't bring her slides," groaned Michael.

After she hung up, Susan pushed open the back door of the kitchen and looked out. The caterer's men had set up long metal tables for the food. The smell of slowly roasting pig radiated from an oblong metal oven on wheels.

Mrs. Brantley stuck her head in the kitchen door. "What a production! I'm never doing *this* again. Never. And you can remind me I said that. Have they got those lanterns up yet? I don't want them to leave that until the last minute. They'll end up climbing all over people."

"I'll check." Susan stepped outside, feeling a sudden catch of happiness in her throat. The sky was full of sunshine, and the leaves of the dogwood trees trembled in a breeze that cast moving shadows on the white-clad tables. It was easy to believe her party would be everything she had hoped, the perfect start to the perfect year.

That evening Ann Lee was getting dressed for the party. She put on an oversize Hard Rock Cafe sweatshirt and then squeezed herself into a pair of skintight black jeans she had bought in Belgium. She examined her image critically in the full-length mirror. A year ago she would never have chosen to wear such a casual outfit to a party, but it was just what she needed for tonight. She wanted everyone to know at a glance how much she had changed. She wanted them to see she was nothing like the fearful girl who had set out for Europe just three months earlier. Now she was brimming with maturity and self-confidence. She intended to throw away every blouse she owned that had a Peter Pan collar— also every blouse that had a demure polka-dot bow at the neck. She would replace them with a half-dozen wrinkled T-shirts. She felt that confident.

Her mother appeared at the door to her bedroom. "You aren't going to wear that to a party!"

Ann Lee grabbed at the waistband of her sweatshirt and her eyes flew anxiously to her mother's face. "What's wrong with it?"

"Nothing—if you're planning to wash the car."

"I like it."

"Well, fine, dear. If you like it, that's the important thing. I certainly think you are old enough to make your own decisions."

"All right, then," Ann Lee muttered.

"It's just that I know Margaret has spent a small fortune on this party—caterers, paper streamers, the works. And she's gone to so much trouble! You wouldn't want her to think you couldn't be bothered to change your clothes."

"Mother! I've been dressing myself for months and I've never caused an international incident."

"I know, but seriously, sweetheart, you don't think those jeans are just a tad too tight? Honestly?"

"They're supposed to be tight."

"I just hope you can sit down. Not that I want to tell you what to wear. You're a young woman now and you ought to make your own decisions. I just hate to see you going out of the house looking like a tramp. When I was a girl if somebody went out in jeans like that we would have known just what she was."

"I've got to be going," Ann Lee said desperately.

"You have plenty of time to change. I'm not saying you should, mind you. But if you should happen to feel uncertain about those pants and want to change, I'm sure you have time. Not everybody's going to arrive at the stroke of seven."

Ann Lee was afraid that if she hung around she would find herself stripping off her jeans and putting on pearl earrings and white gloves. "I want to get on over there now, Mom. Susan might need some help." She squeezed past her mother and fled.

Mrs. Smith stood at the front door of the house and watched her run down the walkway. "I'm sure you'll be perfectly fine," she called.

The doubt in her mother's voice sent a chill up Ann Lee's spine. Were the jeans too tight after all? She flexed her knee, testing them.

She knew her mother meant well. That was what made it so tricky. How could you tell somebody to get out of your way when she was only trying to help? When Ann Lee was a toddler, her mother had buckled her into a harness and leash whenever they went to the shopping center. That way she could keep track of Ann Lee even with her arms full. That was years ago, but sometimes Ann Lee still had the sensation of a leash gently tugging on her. She had lived abroad; she had whizzed through the streets of Bruges after dark on the handlebars of a boy's bike; she had been interviewed on the radio—in Flemish! She wondered if her mother would ever realize that she could dress herself.

A number of cars were parked in front of the Brantleys' house, and Ann Lee smelled pork roasting. The neighborhood felt strange to her. Nothing had changed, so it had to be that she was seeing it with new eyes. The Brantleys' stately colonial-style house was far larger than the house in

Belgium where Ann Lee had lived with four generations of the Los family. And the Brantleys' lot was big enough to be a small farm. As she rounded the house she saw that paper lanterns in bright colors had been strung on lines from the eaves of the house to the dogwood trees at the back of the lot. They swayed gently in the breeze.

"Ann Lee!" Susan held out her arms. "You look great! Did you have a good time?"

"I had a wonderful time!" Ann Lee wondered if she should have brought her slides. She did have some truly spectacular shots of Ghent.

"Say something in Flemish!"

Ann Lee's tongue froze and she couldn't summon a single word of Flemish, but it didn't really matter because Susan wasn't listening.

"Blake! Blake, look who's back!"

Blake unfolded himself from a chair on the patio. Ann Lee had almost forgotten how good-looking he was.

"What a tan, huh?" Susan said and made a face at Blake. "It doesn't seem fair, does it?"

"I carted rocks around all summer for a landscaping company in New England," Blake said apologetically.

"*Everybody's* been gone. It's been so *boring* around here lately," cried Susan. "I'm serious! I never had any idea that so many people were going away. I mean, some people were, like, just on vacation, and they'd come in for a couple of weeks, wash their clothes and all, and then they'd go off again to the beach."

Ann Lee, unreasonably, felt guilty about Susan's dull summer. She couldn't forget that it was Susan who had been chosen to live abroad. It was only because Susan had been unwilling to be away from Jesse for so long that Ann Lee, the first alternate, had been sent.

"Wh-where's Jesse?" Ann Lee stammered.

"Can you believe he's still out on that tractor at his uncle's farm? He ought to be along soon, though."

"So how was Belgium?" Blake asked.

Ann Lee lit up. "It was great. This family that I was staying with—"

"There's Jesse!" Susan waved both arms at him. "People are really starting to come now. I'd better circulate."

"I got to be really good friends with the daughter, Denise," Ann Lee went on doggedly. "She was a year older, but—" She became conscious that Blake was looking over her shoulder. When she turned around she saw another bunch of people arriving. Back by the utility shed, some friends of Susan's younger sister were tossing a Frisbee around.

"Rainey's supposed to come," Blake said. "I've been watching, but I don't see any sign of her yet." He patted Ann Lee's shoulder. "I'm glad you had fun in Belgium. You're looking good." He ambled off to get in a better position to catch the first glimpse of Rainey.

Ann Lee supposed she was still suffering from jet lag because she felt vaguely depressed. She sank down onto the nearest chair and stared at a heap of rocks. Years before, Mr. Brantley had attempted to build a rock garden, and now part of the Brantleys' yard looked like a training ground for a lunar landing. She blinked hard, not knowing why she felt as if she might burst into tears. The sound of a motorcycle in the distance grew louder and louder. She looked around and all at once felt a bit better. Michael was the only person she knew who rode a motorcycle.

Michael Dessaseaux was a huge boy who resembled an unmade bed. He was also the only seventeen-year-old Ann Lee knew who was going gray. He had been friendly to her in first grade when boys thought girls were icky and also in the eighth grade when boys spoke only to girls they were dating. Michael had never been locked into conventional social patterns.

His motorcycle roared down the driveway and up to the entrance of the garage. As Ann Lee got up to go meet him, she noticed a small figure in black riding behind him.

Michael pulled off his helmet and strode toward her, his arms open wide. "Ann Lee! Ann Lee, baby! How'd the frogs treat you?"

"I was in Belgium, actually." He squeezed her until her breath was gone. Just as she was beginning to conclude that artificial resuscitation would be required, he dropped her.

"Hey, do you know C.G.?"

Ann Lee looked into C.G.'s angry dark eyes and gulped.

"We met at the Harley dealership," Michael confided. "Believe me, what C.G. doesn't know about the carburetor of a bike isn't worth knowing."

"E-excuse me," stuttered Ann Lee. "I think they've started serving."

As she joined the rapidly forming line to the food tables, Susan grabbed her arm. "Did you see her? C. G. Bowman—at my party! I'd as soon have the chicken pox. Michael asked if he could bring a date. Would you call C.G. a date, Ann Lee?" Susan shot a hostile look over her shoulder.

"Well, she *is* a girl."

"Only technically. We've got to keep an eye on her. I'm

counting on you. I'm going to pass the word to a few people I can trust. You'll help me out, won't you?''

"I'll do my best.'' Ann Lee wondered what Susan expected her to do if C.G. started causing trouble. Give her a karate chop?

"Remember,'' Susan whispered, "if anything awful happens the number to call is nine-one-one.''

Ann Lee reached the serving table and was invited to cut the slice of her choice off the roast pig carcass. When she hesitated, the caterer's man took her plate from her. ''You're not from around here, are you?'' he said kindly. He quickly sliced her a piece of loin, spooned succotash onto the divided paper plate, and slapped a piece of crisp fried cornbread on top. "Never been to a pig pickin' before, have you? I can always tell.''

Ann Lee meekly moved on to pick up her iced tea, but a voice inside her cried indignantly, I was born here! I've been to lots of pig pickin's. She felt hot with mortification at being taken for an outsider. She wanted to turn around and explain to the man that she was a native of these parts. If she looked out of it, it was only because she was suffering from a severe case of jet lag and letdown.

On the flight home she had pictured her friends crowding around her while she held them spellbound with stories of her adventures. What a laugh. She should have remembered that nobody wanted to hear about other people's summer vacations.

Yet already she could see that people were sneaking glances at C. G. Bowman. It didn't seem fair. Coming to the same party as C.G. was like sharing billing with INXS.

Without bothering to look around for someone she knew,

Ann Lee sat down to eat. It seemed pointless to try to tell anyone about Belgium. No one wanted to hear. No one had even noticed her Hard Rock Cafe sweatshirt. I won't give up, though, she told herself grimly. I am different now. Completely different. Sooner or later, they'll all realize it.

Blake was watching for Rainey with some anxiety. He would have given a lot to be sure of his welcome with her. In the spring when they had been going out together, he felt they had an understanding—nothing spoken, but they were close. Then, just last month, while he was working out of state, Michael had called him. "Brace yourself for a shock, man," he had said. According to Michael, in Blake's absence, Tucker and Rainey had become a couple.

Blake wished then that he had dug in his heels when his father came up with that summer job in New England. "Fresh air, beautiful country," his father had insisted. "You'll stay in shape and get a real break from studying." All of Blake's objections had been overridden.

The job had turned out to be a lot of hard work and not much money. His only consolation was that after spending a morning transporting boulders around some old lady's garden, he could sit with his sandwich, watch whales playing offshore, and feel pretty philosophical about having lost Rainey. What will be will be, he had told himself.

It was only since he got home that her loss had truly hit him. Now, driving past places they used to go together, he couldn't forget her. It was like having an aching tooth.

He was afraid to call her. He didn't want to give her the chance to dismiss him with "Oh, I'm going with Tucker now" and a final click of the telephone receiver. If he could only see her, he knew he could manage to put the relationship together again. He could try, anyway.

Just then an ancient car drove up. With a cough and a sputter, its noisy engine died and Rainey climbed out. She was half Indian, and looking at her in the light of early evening, it was easy for Blake to believe that her ancestors had once had a corner on all the real estate in sight. She was small with a distinctive, determined thrust to her chin. Her blue-black hair was drawn back into a single thick braid, and the thin white cotton shirt she wore with her jeans fluttered a bit, lifted by the light breeze. As she came toward him he could see that, in a rare allusion to her father's people, she was wearing Indian seed bead earrings.

She smiled when she saw him and his chest suddenly felt tight and constricted.

"Blake! You've gotten so dark! How did you do it?"

"I turn regularly and baste every fifteen minutes." He smiled. "No, it was just working outside all summer."

"Must've been nice. I've been slaving over a hot stove at McDonald's."

He fell into step beside her, reining in his stride to match hers. The sight of her had knocked the air out of him, and he was trying to catch his breath. He wanted to say, "Why didn't you answer my letters?" but he choked on the words. He supposed he was afraid to hear her answer.

As they rounded the corner of the house, Rainey stopped short. The Japanese lanterns glowed in the dim light, and what looked like a hundred people milled around the backyard under them. A line snaked up to the serving table where men in white hats were dishing up food.

"Imagine knowing so many people! Where does Susan

find them all?'' Rainey clutched at his arm. ''Good grief, is that C. G. Bowman?''

Looking down, Blake caught the fresh scent of Rainey's hair and a drunken feeling began to steal over him. ''Yeah, C.G. came with Michael.''

''Remember what she did to Missy Melinik?'' Rainey shuddered. ''She absolutely creamed her. I thought maybe she'd been sent to reform school after that.''

''I guess even at reform school they have to let people out eventually.''

''It's easy for you to be superior. She's not likely to punch you out. Michael and C.G.! I can't believe it. Michael must be out of his mind.''

''When it comes to Michael's taste in girls I'm past being surprised.'' He grinned, but Rainey wasn't looking at him. He sensed she was keyed up—her eyes restlessly scanned the yard. A sick feeling in the pit of his stomach told him she was looking for Tucker.

''You say C.G. came with Michael?'' she asked. ''I thought Susan said nobody was bringing dates.''

''Then I guess Susan must have invited her.''

''That's very funny.''

Blake stiffened. It wasn't possible, but he had just spotted Tucker's sleek blond head in the crowd. Susan had double-crossed him.

''Why don't we get some food?'' he said quickly.

''Oh, look, there's Tucker!'' Rainey cried.

Blake's heart sank. ''What's going on, Rainey?'' He grabbed both her hands and held them tightly. ''Why didn't you answer my letters?''

"Oh, I don't know." She avoided his eyes. "I guess I'm not much of a letter writer."

"I thought you told me you were going to keep your options open."

"You were away all summer," she said sharply. "Was I supposed to sit around working crossword puzzles?"

"All right, I went away. So you and Tucker had to rush out and get matching tattoos or something?" he said bitterly.

"You don't own me!" she flared.

"Look, you know I didn't mean it that way!" She had already jerked her hands free and was walking away from him.

He managed to keep himself from calling after her, but his throat hurt with the effort. He was sure that if they'd had some time together alone, he could have made it all right, but he had blown it. Rainey was not a girl you could push.

Susan jogged over to him, looking apprehensive.

"You promised me!" He gritted his teeth. "Now I know who I can count on, don't I?"

"It's not my fault, Blake! Honest, it's not! When my mom was talking to Tucker's mom she found out Tucker never got an invitation and she told his mother it must have been lost in the mail. I didn't even know about it. She only just told me. I'm sorry. What's going on, anyway? Is Rainey mad at you or something?"

"Or something," he said flatly. He felt like hitting somebody, but instead he turned and walked away.

Mrs. Brantley pulled up a chair next to Ann Lee. "Can you believe Tucker's invitation got lost in the mail? Luckily I happened to run into his mother and I was able to straighten it all out. I was just telling Susan. So tell me, dear, how was Belgium? I want to hear *all* about it."

"It was a wonderful experience!" Ann Lee spoke in a rush. "At first I was homesick, you know? And I had to work so hard just to get a little basic knowledge of the language. Mrs. Los was a real help with that. Every night we would go over my lessons. But the really incredible thing was how free I felt! You can't imagine what it was like! Because I was in a different country and spoke a different language, I wasn't the same person I am here. Do you know what I mean?"

"I wish Susan had taken advantage of that wonderful opportunity," said Mrs. Brantley distractedly. "What memories you'll have!"

"Absolutely. You know, I don't think I'll ever be the same again." But the truth was that every hour she was home she could feel her confidence slipping. What good was it to change inside if everyone treated her just the same?

Ann Lee followed Mrs. Brantley's gaze and saw she was eyeing Jesse. "You know, I don't like big parties," Susan's mother said. "I always think that no amount of fun is worth having the flower beds trampled."

Ann Lee looked uneasily over her shoulder. So far the peonies next to the house appeared to be untrampled. The trellis of climbing roses, check. She glanced at the zinnias in the cutting garden. Intact as far as she could see. She decided Mrs. B. was speaking figuratively.

"I just thought that Susan ought to stay in touch with her friends," Mrs. Brantley said. "It seems as if Jesse's the only person she ever sees these days. It's such a mistake to let yourself get cut off from everyone else because you're wrapped up in a boy. I let her have this party because I thought it would make her realize what she's missing. I like Jesse, of course, but it would be better if she dated more than one boy.''

Ann Lee was feeling more inadequate by the moment. She didn't even have one boyfriend, and now Mrs. Brantley seemed to be saying that every self-respecting girl should have a stable of them.

"Excuse me, dear." Mrs. Brantley stood up. "I think I'd better go confiscate that Frisbee. I don't want it landing on somebody's plate.''

Blake sat down next to Ann Lee, looking grim.

She eyed him uneasily. Somehow she sensed that he had not sought her out to hear about her experience in Belgium. "Did you find Rainey yet?"

"Yeah, she's here. Has Rainey said anything about me to you, Ann Lee?"

"Uh, I just flew in last night, remember?"

"Oh, right. I forgot.''

Everybody had forgotten, she thought dismally.

"You know if I really thought she and Tucker belonged together, if I really thought that, it would be different." A plastic fork snapped in Blake's hands.

"I've got a spare." Ann Lee's eyes flew anxiously to his face. She handed him the fork.

He scraped off the little bits of white plastic that littered his plate. "Jeez, Rainey and I have known each other forever. Tucker sweeps in here, feeds her a line, and she acts like it's the Second Coming. I mean, give me a break.''

"A person can get taken for granted, all right." Ann Lee felt as if her words had been wrung from bitter experience.

"Tell me something," he said suddenly. "If a person does a big favor for another person, do you think that person ought to hold it against them?"

Ann Lee looked at him blankly. "Come again?"

"Last year I did Rainey this big favor, you see?"

"You did? What kind of favor?"

His eyes shifted. "Actually, I lent her some money. She paid me back, but ever since then, the least little thing and she gets the idea I'm lording it over her."

"Gratitude can be tough to handle."

"I wish I'd never offered her the bleeping money, that's for sure." White plastic shards spattered his plate again.

"Let me get you another fork." She leapt up, waving away his protests. "No, really, don't worry about it. I was getting up anyway."

At the serving table Ann Lee collected a slice of chocolate cake and five white plastic forks. At the rate Blake was going through them she figured she needed more than just a few. She was turning to go back to her place when she heard a commotion behind her.

"Don't be stupid, C.G. Cut it out!"

"You're going to break your neck. Stop it!"

When Ann Lee wheeled around, she spotted C.G. scrambling up the rose trellis attached to the back of the house. A sharp cracking noise sounded, but just as the trellis gave way, one last leap took C.G. to the roof. The broken trellis sagged against the wall, its roses starting to wilt already.

Ann Lee heard Mrs. Brantley's muffled scream.

"Get down from there instantly, young lady." Mr. Brantley was pink in the face. He would have looked comical with his white legs sticking out of his Bermuda shorts, if he hadn't been so frighteningly angry. "You're going to hurt yourself."

"Maybe I can fly." C.G. was standing defiantly, feet apart, on the edge of the roof. From the flash of her white teeth in the dusk, Ann Lee knew C.G. was enjoying herself. You had to hand it to her, Ann Lee thought. She certainly knew how to get attention.

"Oh, no," Susan moaned. "My poor party."

"Should we call the fire department?" asked a froggy voice behind Ann Lee. "That's what we did when my cat went up on the roof."

"Okay, C.G., you've made your point," said Michael. "Now come on down."

"Catch!" yelled C.G. She threw out her arms and leapt off the roof.

She fell into Michael's outstretched arms. "Oomph," he grunted, reeling.

Ann Lee could hear people exhaling all around her. She felt rather limp herself.

"What's she on?" somebody behind Ann Lee asked.

"C.G. doesn't have to be on anything," another voice replied. "That's just the way she is."

When Ann Lee looked back at the patio, Michael had his arm around C.G., though whether to support or restrain her, Ann Lee couldn't determine. He gave a quick glance around at the horrified faces of the guests. "Well, I guess we'd better be getting you on home, C.G. Terrific party, Mr. Brantley. 'Bye, Susan. Love those Japanese lanterns, Mrs. Brantley. So long."

Ann Lee wondered what had possessed Michael to bring C.G. to the party in the first place. Where was the attraction?

She wished she had a brother who could help her understand the workings of the male mind. It was no use asking her father. There was no similarity whatsoever between her father and the boys of West Mount High. Her father wore rimless bifocals and pin-striped suits and was very particular about his favorite chair and about the newspaper not being messed up. She felt pretty sure that Michael's interest in C.G. would be as much a mystery to him as it was to her.

She took her chocolate cake back to her table and sat down. "Wow, that was something, wasn't it?"

Blake looked up. "What?"

"You didn't see it?"

"See what?"

Ann Lee heard the roar of Michael's departing motorcycle. "Never mind," she said. "Here are your forks."

"The thing is," Blake went on relentlessly. "Tucker can't tell one girl from another. Every summer when he came home from prep school it was like flipping through the *Sports Illustrated* swimsuit issue—just a blur of blondes."

"Rainey's not a blonde," Ann Lee pointed out. "Maybe he's maturing."

Blake glared at her.

"I mean, you're absolutely right," she amended hastily. "I see what you mean exactly. It is weird the way he swooped down on her like that. It kind of makes you wonder."

"It makes me wonder if he went after her just to get at me."

She was taken aback. "Aren't you being a little paranoid?"

"Okay, I'm paranoid. Paranoiacs can have real enemies, you know."

Susan made her way through the crowd to their table. She sat down beside Ann Lee, her eyes tragic. "Can you believe it? My party, the *only* big party my mother has ever let me have and probably the *last* one she'll ever let me have, is going to go down in history as the one where C. G. Bowman tried to fly!"

"What?" Blake was bewildered.

"You mean you didn't see it, Blake?" Susan looked at him incredulously. "She *jumped right off the roof!*"

"Is she hurt?"

"Don't I wish! No, I take that back. I don't really wish she was hurt. Not at my house. I just wish she hadn't come to my party. There is only one bright spot to this, one teensy little bright spot—I do *not* think my mom will ask me to be nice to C.G. anymore."

Ann Lee had given up trying to tell anyone about her adventures in Belgium. It was clearly a hopeless quest. All anybody would talk about now was C.G. She lifted her eyes and watched a white moth futilely bat its wings against the paper lantern overhead. It looked as if breaking in a new identity was going to be more difficult than she had thought.

THREE

Sunday afternoon Michael sat sprawled in Blake's room leafing through a guide to colleges.

"Get this," he said. "It says, 'The students at this rigorous technical school have a well-earned reputation for playing practical jokes.' "

Blake lifted an eyebrow. "Run that by me again. A rigorous technical college—*you?*"

"Shut up. I'm just getting to the good part. Listen— 'During one well-remembered football game, the school's whiz kids sent a radio-controlled hot air balloon over to the visiting team's bench, where it exploded on command, showering the opposing players with baby powder.' I've got to tell C.G. about that. She probably knows exactly how they did it. I tell you, Blake, the girl is amazing. She fixed my carburetor—like that." He snapped his fingers.

"I'm happy for you."

"Look, just because Rainey dumped you is no reason to be down on everybody."

"I'll remember that."

"Whew! It says this place has a six-to-one boy-girl ratio. Forget that. Why would anybody want to go to a school like that?"

Blake flipped a potato chip up and caught it in his mouth, but that small feat didn't seem to cheer him any. "Did I tell you my dad wants me to apply to Princeton?"

"Well, you might be able to get in. You're smart."

"Not that smart."

"I, on the other hand, plan to apply to Dogpatch U. or any similarly illustrious institution where they have a film studies program." Michael stretched until the chair he was sitting in squeaked in protest. "Finally, a reward for all those hours I spent in dark theaters when I should have been doing algebra."

"You're sure laid back enough about this college stuff."

"It's C.G. I give her all the credit. I've got more to think about these days than college applications, Blake old bean. I'm crazy about that girl. I've never met anybody like her. She's unique. The fire! The passion!"

"Let's keep it clean."

"Believe me, Blake, under all that black leather is a truly womanly woman."

Blake counted backward slowly from ten, hoping the impulse to say something nasty about C.G. would leave him. "But seriously," he said at last, "it doesn't drive you nuts the way she keeps stubbing out one cigarette after another?

I thought when people quit smoking they didn't want to be around all that. I thought it brought on the urge.''

"Me? Nah, heck, I like it. In fact, when I kiss her there's this smoky taste to her mouth—it kind of does something to me, you know?''

"That isn't love, man. That's a nicotine fit.''

"Don't knock it. It works for me. Hey, did I tell you? C.G.'s going to pierce my ear for me.''

"Pierce your *ear?*'' Blake sat up straight. "Are you serious?''

"Hey, man, everybody does it now.''

"Not around here, they don't. Name me one guy who's got a pierced ear!''

"How do you think I'd look with a thin gold hoop?''

"Queer.''

"All right, Farraby, watch it! C.G. thinks earrings are sexy on men. She likes the idea of a single gold cross. But I see myself as more the classic type—plain gold hoop. What do you think?''

"The cross would come in handy if you run into any vampires.''

"True. Clearly this is something I'm going to have to give a lot of deep thought to.''

"Yeah, you'd better think it over for a year or two at least, that's my opinion.'' Blake stared moodily out the window. There was a moment of silence. Finally he said, "I'm going to call Carmen Harper.''

"Nice girl, Carmen.''

"I don't want Rainey to think I'm completely wiped out over this, you know?''

"Yeah, there are a lot more where she came from.''

"I don't want to sit around looking pitiful. I mean the last thing I want is for her to feel sorry for me. It would really get me down if I thought she felt that way."

"Blake, listen carefully. This is your best friend speaking. You can believe what I say. Nobody feels sorry for you. I mean, nobody. Not Rainey. Nobody. Zip. *Nada*. Zero persona."

"Well, good. I guess."

"Look, you drive a new red Corvette, you're smart, you look good. I don't say that you're my type or anything, but I've seen the little girls swooning over you down by the tennis courts."

"Cut it out," Blake mumbled.

"Seriously, it amazes me how people can see themselves in the mirror for, say, seventeen or even forty years and not have the foggiest idea what they look like. My dad thinks he's a handsome devil and here you think you're ugly. Go figure."

"Well, maybe not ugly, exactly. Just your fairly ordinary kind of guy."

"Right. Well, that's what I'm talking about." Michael brightened. "Gosh, just think if it was possible to trade looks, I could offer to switch with you *if* you threw in the Corvette and you'd probably snap up the deal in a minute! It's an idea! I think I'm onto something here. Of course, I've got a few technical details to iron out with the mind-body exchange."

"Maybe C.G. could help you out with the technical details."

Blake's sarcasm bounced off Michael. "Maybe so. She's

one sharp girl, believe me. I'll mention it to her." Michael flipped the pages of the college guide.

"My dad wants me to take one of those courses they give to build up your SAT scores," Blake said.

"Jeez, I thought your scores were great. My parents *loved* your scores."

"But what about Princeton?"

"Princeton might not be as impressed as my parents," Michael conceded.

"If I took that course, I'd have to go all the way to Raleigh three, maybe four times a week. I don't know if I'll do it or not. Of course, when it comes down to it, I may have to go whether I want to or not. You know my dad."

" 'Yes, master, I won't do it again!' " Michael writhed in his chair. " 'Don't hit me! Please, please, anything but— the treatment!' "

Blake grinned. "He's not that bad."

Michael propped his feet up on Blake's bed. "Well, let me know how you like Carmen, okay? I bet you two will get along great."

"If she goes out with me, you mean."

"Blake, Blake, she will go out with you. And she's your type. More than Rainey, I mean. Rainey drives this independence bit into the ground, in my opinion. She's the type that's always going to be telling you what to do. Now, this Carmen is different. She's a soft, sweet girl. I like her."

That was the difference between Michael and him, thought Blake. Michael was always thinking about whether he liked the girl, whereas Blake was always thinking about whether the girl liked *him*. If he could trade anything with

Michael, that would have been it; he wished he had a quarter of Michael's confidence.

School began the next day. Everyone had on new shoes and bounced around hugging friends. Blake did not share in the general effervescence. What he noticed most was that the new books he'd been issued weighed a ton. When he thought of the school year stretching before him, he felt more tired than anything. "You want to try to get calculus out of the way," his father had said. Why? So he could take something even harder in college? He did not always follow his father's logic.

On top of it all, there was the problem with Rainey. By lunchtime Blake was about to crack from the strain of knowing that around any corner he might run into her. Or Tucker. He didn't know which would be worse. He was afraid that if Tucker gave him that smug, superior look of his, he might just lose it entirely and drop a ton of books on the guy's head. It was doubtful that Princeton would like the looks of that on his permanent record.

It had been easier during the summer. He hadn't had to think about Rainey and Tucker every minute. He could play tennis or haul boulders until he was too tired to think straight. But when he was at school he couldn't get away from them.

By the end of the day, Blake was sure he had aged visibly. He actually checked out his reflection in a mirror when he got home and was surprised to see no change. Probably it was impossible for a deeply tanned face to look haggard, but he sure as heck felt haggard. No doubt his health would break later.

After supper he called Carmen Harper. "Carmen?"

"Yes?" Her voice was cautious, which he found mildly discouraging.

"This is Blake. Blake Farraby."

There was a loud clunk. Blake held the receiver away from his ear, then tried again. "Carmen?"

"Oh, I'm so sorry. I— The phone just slipped out of my hand, I don't know why. This is so stupid. I think maybe it's because my brother's always tangling up the phone cord, playing with it, you know?"

"Those phones can take on a life of their own, all right." She giggled.

"So, what do you think of French this year?"

"It looks—well, it seems like a lot of homework. To me, I mean. I guess it doesn't seem like a lot of work to someone like you."

"It's a lot of reading."

"Yeah."

"Are we having trouble with this connection or something? I can hardly hear you."

"Oh! I guess that's just me. Sometimes I don't talk loud enough. My father's always telling me not to mumble. I'll try to talk louder."

"I can hear you okay now. Well, the reason I'm calling, is I kind of wondered if you'd like to go to a play at the college on Friday night. I don't know if it'll be any good. Or maybe you don't even like plays or anything. Or we could go to a movie. But maybe you're busy."

"Oh, that sounds—"

A loud clunk sounded in his ear. She had dropped the receiver again.

"Oh, this is so embarrassing!" she said and giggled again. "I can't believe I did that. The phone must be—slippery—or something."

"It's okay," Blake said hastily. "Don't worry about it. So is it all settled, then? I'll pick you up Friday night, maybe at seven. Okay?"

"That would be great. Just lovely. I mean, I'd like that. Well, anyway, you know what I mean."

Blake dropped the receiver back into its cradle and breathed deeply. He couldn't believe he had just committed himself to spend an entire evening with this girl. He was practically in a cold sweat after talking to her for three minutes.

"She likes you, Blake old boy. Trust me," Michael said the next day. "She got flustered when you told her who it was, didn't she? It means she likes you. That's why she kept dropping the phone. Nerves."

They filed into English class. A woman with tight gray curls was sitting at the desk.

"A substitute," said Michael, perking up.

"Mrs. Philpot's daughter just had a baby." Bitsy Ferguson always knew that sort of thing. She had some kind of invisible antennae that picked up even the feeblest grapevine signal.

Michael took the desk ahead of C.G. She immediately rested her head against his broad back and twined her arms around him. Blake felt a twinge of envy. It would be nice to really belong to somebody that way. Particularly if the somebody was Rainey, but he couldn't think about her now.

"Class, I hope we all know how to behave like ladies and gentlemen." The substitute teacher glared at C.G. and Michael. "I am not going to put up with any nonsense. I want that understood from the outset."

Blake recognized this statement as the identifying call of the teacher who could not maintain order. He had learned from experience that the worse teachers were at discipline the more they blustered at the beginning of class.

The rest of the class had obviously already taken the substitute's measure. A spitball hit Blake's ear.

"Mrs. Philpot anticipated her absence," the substitute said tensely. "I have her lesson plan and some exercises you are to do." She began passing out mimeographed sheets.

"Look, Mikey," said C.G. "I remembered!"

Blake glanced over and saw that C.G. was holding out a cork. Protruding from it was a glistening needle.

"I can do it right here," said C.G.

"Right here? Shouldn't you have alcohol or something?" asked Michael.

"The needle's sterile. No problem."

"C.G.'s going to pierce Michael's ear!" Bitsy reported ecstatically.

"What?" Blake stared.

"Can't you see? She's got a needle," said Bitsy.

"My God!"

A murmur ran around the room.

"What are you two doing over there?" the substitute cried.

"I'm piercing his ear," said C.G.

"You can't do that here!"

Michael flinched as C.G. drove the needle through his earlobe. A drop of blood fell onto the gray tile floor.

Harvey Klein slumped in his seat.

"Harvey's fainted!" Bitsy shouted.

Blake jumped up from his seat.

"Put his head down!" advised Susannah Morely.

"Check his tongue. Maybe he's swallowed his tongue!"

Blake bent over him anxiously as he stirred. "Are you all right, Harvey?"

"Fine," Harvey said in a blurry voice. He sounded as if he was just waking up. "Go 'way." He leaned forward, closed his eyes, and rested his head on his hands.

The substitute had turned white. "Maybe you'd better go see the nurse," she whispered. "I suppose there is a school nurse, isn't there? Or you could go to the office. I'll give you an office pass." She snatched pieces of paper at random from Mrs. Philpot's desk.

"What if he faints on the way to the office?" Bitsy said. "I'd better go with him, just to keep an eye on him. He might go into shock or even have a fit or something."

"I'm okay. Just leave me alone. The sight of blood does this to me." Harvey was red in the face.

"Just dab it with alcohol several times a day," C.G. told Michael.

Blake saw that Michael's earlobe had a plain gold stud in it, and except for the drop of blood on the tile floor there was nothing to show that his earlobe had ever been any other way. Blake was glad he hadn't passed out like Harvey because the truth was that the idea of sticking a needle through that soft flesh made him feel queasy. The things girls figured out to do! He decided that whoever called them the weaker sex must have had a weird sense of humor.

The substitute popped some little white pills under her tongue.

"Are you okay, ma'am?" asked Bitsy brightly.

"I'm fine." The teacher swallowed. "I just have a slight heart condition."

"Watch out, C.G.," Brian Hadley intoned in a deep voice. "This could be murder one."

C.G. turned on him venomously. "Get lost, Brian."

Blake touched Michael's arm. "You aren't feeling light-headed or anything, are you? Because if you go down, man, it'll make quite a crash. I mean, lives could be lost."

"Chill out, Blake old buddy. It's nothing. Worse things than this happen in wartime."

After that, Blake fiddled with his pencil and avoided looking at the dark spot of blood on the floor. His best friend had a pierced ear. His best girl was going with somebody else. In his wildest fantasies he had never dreamed senior year would be as bad as this.

FOUR

_T_ucker rolled his program into a tube and peered through it to survey the auditorium. "There are enough people here tonight."

"I expect their English teachers made them come," said Rainey.

"I guess you're right. Everybody I see looks like a student here at the college. No, I take that back—not everybody."

Rainey followed his gaze and saw Blake and Carmen filing into seats across the aisle. She looked down at once and pretended to study her program. "Playgoers will remember Biff Meadows as Shylock in the college's spring production of _The Merchant of Venice_," she read. "When not involved in thespian pursuits, Mr. Meadows enjoys water skiing and making rope hammocks." Rope hammocks? They had to be kidding.

Her brow puckered unhappily. She didn't like to think that Blake was mad at her, but he probably was. And she couldn't really blame him. As soon as she saw him at Susan's party, she knew she should have told him about Tucker but just couldn't make herself do it. She couldn't find the words. She wasn't sure whether that was because she dreaded hurting his feelings or what. Seeing him there had startled her and knocked her into a state of complete confusion. She had panicked. All she could do was look around for Tucker to rescue her. She didn't want Blake to demand an explanation. She didn't have an explanation.

Becoming Tucker's girlfriend had seemed natural. The world was set up like Noah's Ark with everyone expected to be paired off. It was only now, seeing Blake with Carmen, that Rainey found herself trying to remember how it had happened. She still felt funny about it. How could she explain to Blake how he had gotten squeezed out of her life when she wasn't sure how it had happened herself?

After Blake left town early in the summer, she had seen more and more of Tucker. Then one evening over pizza, Tucker had said, "This isn't just fun and games, Rainey. I'm serious. I want you to be my girl." He had looked directly into her eyes, and Rainey felt herself melting inside. She felt so flattered that he had chosen her. "*I* don't want to go out with anybody else," he had said. All at once she was struck with the absolute certainty that she didn't want to go out with anyone else, either.

The two of them spent a lot of time together after that. One weekend she got someone to fill in for her at work and she went with Tucker's family to their cedar-shingled beach house at the Outer Banks. She loved it. It was so far away from the hot kitchens of McDonald's and the thin walls and petty economies of home. No one worked at the Harbissons' beach house, and yet the refrigerator was always full of expensive food—fresh cherries and real butter and T-bone streaks. She and Tucker played volleyball on the beach, flew kites, and got sunburned shoulders. The sound of the surf echoed in Rainey's ears all day, and at night the waves seemed to rock her as she slept with mosquitoes buzzing outside the window screen. It was hot and she was seventeen and tired of trying. She felt as if she were floating, with no plans and no memory.

She could feel herself letting go of the drive to succeed that had always been pulled tight inside her like a rubber band. She wondered sometimes if she was borrowing part of Tucker's personality. Maybe that was the way it worked. Maybe that was why long-married people grew to look and walk alike.

Later in the summer, one lazy afternoon, she and Tucker had floated down a river in inner tubes. Tucker was naturally drawn to water. He liked fishing and messing around in boats and any kind of water sport. The gnats gathered in a cloud around their eyes, and their skin itched as the water on their legs dried in the sunshine. Tucker floated a bucket of iced drinks on an inner tube beside them. He sang "Old Man River" over and over again until finally Rainey surprised even herself when she chimed in with her husky contralto. She was no singer, but it didn't seem to matter. When she was with Tucker she didn't have to be good at anything. It was enough just to be.

On the Fourth of July Rainey and Tucker had shared a blanket during the city fireworks display. The starbursts exploding overhead had suited her exultant mood. It had amazed her that two people who were so different had found each other.

She knew she wasn't his first girl. She had seen snapshots in his family album of girls called Traci, Bobbi, Susi, Bambi—blondes with no last names, their faces slightly out of focus. They didn't bother her. They were in the past.

Beside her in the dimly lit theater, Tucker rattled his program. "Nice," he whispered in her ear.

Rainey glanced up to see a blonde showing an elderly couple to their seats near the front. The girl deposited the couple and glided back up the aisle, clutching a handful of programs. She had matching dimples on either side of a sweet mouth. Rainey racked her brain trying to remember why she looked so familiar. Did she work at the dry cleaners? The bank? Then something clicked into place and Rainey realized she didn't know the girl at all. She was noticing the resemblance to the snapshots of Tucker's old girlfriends. Suddenly uneasy, she shot a sharp look at Tucker.

He smiled. "I do appreciate a good-looking girl—present company included, of course." He tapped his program absently against the back of the seat in front of him. "Hey, who's that over there with Blake?"

Rainey closed her program. "Carmen something-or-other. She moved here a couple of years ago when you were still away at prep school."

"She must have made a big impression on you if you can't even remember her last name."

"She doesn't talk very much. I think she's shy."

"Well, she's full of herself tonight. Look at her."

Rainey didn't want to look. It was none of her business

46

who Blake was with, but she was curious. Carmen's cheeks were pink with excitement. In fact, she looked quite pretty.

"She's probably beside herself being asked out by the great Blake Farraby," said Tucker. "She's probably been salivating all over his Corvette all night."

"So what if she has?" Rainey said. "What's wrong with her enjoying herself?"

"Forget I said it. I take it all back."

"Anybody would think you didn't like Blake." As soon as the words were out of her mouth, she felt slightly foolish. Why did she want to believe that Tucker and Blake liked each other? It was so obvious they didn't.

"Not like Blake-nice-guy-honor-student Farraby? I thought that was against the law."

A new and interesting idea suddenly occurred to Rainey. "You couldn't be a little bit jealous of him, could you?"

"Ouch! You got it in one."

"But that's just silly! Why would you be jealous? What does he have that you don't?" Even as she spoke, she began thinking of things Blake had that Tucker didn't—ambition and energy and sensitivity, to name three. She had to force herself to stop. It was ridiculous to compare them. They were two completely different people, that was all.

"What does he have?" Tucker pretended to think. "Well, there's— and there's—" He grinned. "Nope, I'm not going to tell you. It's like some beautiful girl who says she's always hated her tiny eyes. Instead of thinking how gorgeous she is, you end up thinking, 'Gee, her eyes really *are* tiny.' I think I'll just keep my ideas to myself."

"You're perfectly okay, Tucker."

"I know. I'm wonderful. Keep it up. I definitely need a

47

cheering section. Good grief, look over there. I swear that girl's mouth hasn't stopped moving for a single second. What can she be saying? It looks like she's giving a play-by-play account of a Ping-Pong match.''

Rainey would have preferred to forget that Blake was even there. If Tucker hadn't pointed him out, she thought ruefully, she wouldn't have noticed. Now she was going to be uneasy all evening.

To Rainey's relief, the house lights dimmed and the curtain went up. The stage was decorated like a topiary, with trees shaped like giant green lollipops. Young men in tights and doublets strode onstage while a couple of mustached fiddlers sawed away energetically at their instruments.

''If music be the food of love, play on!'' cried the player in the red doublet.

Rainey had been looking forward to seeing *Twelfth Night*, but something was wrong with her concentration. The first line of the play kept repeating in her mind like a broken record—food of love, love, love.

She didn't like the way Tucker had admired the blond usher, though she tried to convince herself that her reaction was immature. Above all, she wished she hadn't seen Blake. She felt miserably guilty about snapping at him the night of Susan's party. Maybe what was bothering her was that she had never been properly grateful to him for the time he had lent her money. She hadn't liked taking money from him, but she could have been more gracious about it. She was conscious that she could have been nicer all around, but it wasn't easy for her.

When Rainey was twelve, her father had dropped out of sight, leaving the household disastrously short of money.

Her mother had had to sell their dining table and chairs to a secondhand shop to get money for the week's food, and the mother of a classmate had brought over some outgrown clothes and a large rib roast to help out. Rainey's mom couldn't understand why Rainey wasn't happy about the clothes. "There's lots of wear in them yet," she had pointed out. She hadn't realized that everyone at school would recognize Felicia's old clothes and would know why Rainey was wearing them. Rainey had never been able to forget what it was like to be the object of charity—it was humiliating.

These days Rainey's mother earned a steady income working as a waitress at the Carolina Bar and Grill, and Rainey was able to help out with a part-time job of her own. They lived in an old trailer at the edge of town where lot rents were cheap. They ate regularly and Rainey had some nice clothes, though not with designer labels. They got along okay.

It had been a painful step back into the past when Rainey's father showed up the past February and March needing money to get out of town. Blake had figured out what was going on, although Rainey never was entirely clear how he'd done it. That was the way it was with him—sometimes he read her mind. He obviously knew how she felt about the loan because he never mentioned it again. Still, Rainey couldn't get it out of her mind. Every time she thought of it, it reminded her of Felicia's clothes.

The humiliation of those old days rushed back to her now. With panic rising in her throat, she felt unsteady as if the floor of the theater were giving way. All at once she was struck with the bitter certainty that Tucker was going to leave her the way her father had. The happy days of summer were slipping away, and a cold vision of the future left her gasping.

Tucker nuzzled her neck. "I hate culture, don't you?"

"Shhh," someone behind them hissed.

Tucker made a face. "I bet they're taking notes for class. Wake me when it's over." He winced. "Listen to that stuff. You'd think they'd at least have subtitles!"

He rested his head on her shoulder and Rainey watched her breath ruffle his fair hair. She was comforted by his closeness. Her sudden panic attack didn't have anything to do with him, she told herself. At least she was bright enough to see that, even if she was shaken at the moment.

She tried to listen to the tale of Illyria, the never-never land in Shakespeare's play. It was good to have something to occupy her mind, she told herself. Tucker looked half asleep; she wondered if he was even listening to the play. It was his kind of thing. It had an antipuritanical message that could have passed for his personal philosophy. In fact, if he were wearing a doublet and had a paunch, he could have made a fairly decent Sir Toby Belch.

Rainey found the effort of keeping her mind on the play tiring. When at last the actors took their curtain calls, her scalp was tight with tension.

The house lights went up, and she grabbed Tucker's hand. "Whaa?" he grunted.

"Let's go. Come on." She edged out of her seat and began pressing her way through the crowd.

"Hold up, Rainey." He struggled to catch up. "Where's the fire?"

"I thought we'd try to beat the crowd. I don't like to be the last one out."

She kept her eyes straight ahead, afraid of catching a glimpse of Blake as she marched through the crowd and outside to Tucker's car. It was a cool night, and the fresh air smelled good. Rainey took a deep breath and decided she felt better.

They drove to Feno's coffee shop. There they sat in the back booth and waited for their order while Rainey traced a path on the cracked Formica with her finger. She tried not to think. She felt as if she was at a crossroads, but she wasn't sure why. It was only this crazy stuff going on in her mind. Nothing had happened—really. And maybe nothing would happen. People had moods, that was all. Quite possibly, if she took vitamins or began jogging, it would go away. She only wanted things to go on as they had been. That didn't seem like a lot to ask.

The waitress brought cups of coffee and pastries.

"Sheesh, I'm tired." Tucker pressed his fingers against his closed eyes and stretched his legs out under the table. He yawned, then tilted the sugar dispenser and watched as a Niagara of sugar fell into his cup. He liked his coffee syrupy. "Do you think we could get Mrs. Philpot to give us extra credit for going to see that play?" he asked. "It ought to be good for something."

Rainey curled a leg under her. "I don't understand why we went if you didn't want to see it."

"My parents had tickets. They belong to this Friends of the College thing, and they get season tickets to all the events, but they hardly ever go. The plays are usually on a weeknight and my dad says he's too tired to go anywhere then."

"But still—"

"We could have gone to see *The Slumber Party Massacre* at Park Street Cinema! Gee!" He snapped his fingers. "I didn't think of it."

"Well, what *were* you thinking of?" Rainey said in exasperation. Tucker's inclination to take the path of least resistance still surprised her sometimes.

"I don't know. I just had these tickets, you know."

She reminded herself that Tucker's laid-back approach to life definitely had its advantages. She didn't have to worry about his offering her alfalfa while he was on some natural foods kick, for instance, and he never scolded her for having opinions different from his. Tucker was not very much interested in opinions. He was more concerned with boats, horses, and good food. She tried to remember if they had ever had a serious conversation. She didn't think so.

"Next time I suggest going to some cultural event," he said, "stop me. I have had enough culture to last me, oh, ten years or so." He grabbed her hand. "Rainey, do you like me?"

She looked at him with startled eyes. "You know I like you!"

"Yes, but do you just have-a-good-time like me or do you love-type like me?"

"Could you run that by me again? Oh, don't be silly, Tucker. You know I like you." She felt suddenly on edge, and she had lost her appetite for the pastry. She wanted to leave and sort out her thoughts in the privacy of her own room.

"I'm just crazy about you. Grrrrr," he growled, his eyes half closed. "Let's go park the car in the woods somewhere. The deep, dark woods."

"I'd love to." She scrambled out from the booth. "But I've got to get home. I've got to be at work at six-thirty tomorrow."

"Work, work, work—since school started, all you do is work."

"I'm sorry about that."

"Oh, I didn't mean anything. Don't flash those eyes at me, okay? Let's go."

Monday at lunch Rainey stood near the trash bin holding her tray and scanning the cafeteria uncertainly. It felt strange to be looking for someone to eat with. She and Tucker had eaten together every single day since school started. At first she saw only tables filled with strangers, but then finally she spotted Ann Lee sitting by herself.

Ann Lee was surprised when Rainey sat down with her. "Gee, Rainey, long time no see. Where's Tucker?"

"He's having speech therapy over at the hospital."

Ann Lee's mouth feel open. "He is! What happened? Has he been in an accident or something? He looked fine last time I saw him."

Rainey shook her head. "He used to stutter when he was little, and now when he's tired he says it's started to come back. He may have to miss lunch altogether for the next few weeks.''

"A really intensive course of treatment, huh?''

"I guess so.'' Rainey tore her milk carton open. It wouldn't have mattered that she had to find someone new to eat lunch with except that the logical people for her to sit with—Ann Lee, Susan, Michael—were exactly the same ones Blake usually sat with, and it made her nervous to think that at any minute he might come over. In one way, she'd be glad to see him, to put right any misunderstanding. It seemed important to make him see that she wasn't mad at him. That was the least she could do. Actually, she knew the issue would never arise. Once he saw her at a table, he'd sit somewhere else. She'd never see him at all, most likely.

Susan walked up just then and dropped her tray on the table with a clatter. Jesse sat down across from her. "It's only the second week of school, and already I've remembered all the things I hate about it. Like the food.''

"The hamburgers aren't so bad,'' put in Jesse.

"Jesse will eat anything,'' said Susan. "Don't listen to him.''

Rainey removed her hamburger from her bun and looked at it suspiciously. The meat looked shiny, as if the kitchen staff had zapped it with spray varnish. She wondered if the calories saved by not eating the bun were a fair trade-off for having to confront the meat directly. Clearly there were some things you were better off not facing, and this hamburger was one of them.

"I think they put oatmeal in them,'' Ann Lee said. "That's why they look funny.''

"Nah, I bet it's arsenic.'' Susan grinned at Jesse.

Susan and Jesse looked so happy with each other that Rainey had the impulse to ask them outright whether either of them ever felt drawn to other people. She really would have liked to know.

The whole business of love was so hard for her to understand. She distinctly remembered wanting to fall in love, but she had imagined it would be some sort of permanent acquisition, rather like one of Susan's gold chains. Now it seemed more like fleeting light caught in a mirror. It could dazzle her eyes one minute, but if she turned the mirror the slightest bit, it was gone. Was it this way with everyone or was there something wrong with her?

She wasn't sure how she felt about Tucker. She couldn't seem to catch hold of the feeling she'd had before, and yet she knew it must be there somewhere. One minute she'd be thinking how attractive Tucker was, and the next minute, slightly annoyed, she'd be counting his personal flaws. What did that mean? She just wished she knew how these things were with other people.

"Susan, do you remember when Tucker stuttered?"

Ann Lee's question scattered Rainey's thoughts, and she found herself listening for Susan's answer.

"Tucker?" Susan frowned. "No . . . wait a minute. It seems like in kindergarten he did sort of stutter. I remember Billy Tomkins used to make fun of him."

"Oh, I remember Billy Tomkins!" exclaimed Ann Lee. "He pasted toilet paper all over the walls of the bathroom in the second grade. After that he sort of disappeared. I wonder whatever happened to Billy."

"He got five to ten in Sing Sing." Rainey stabbed her hamburger with her fork.

"Really?"

Susan rolled her eyes. "Honestly, Ann Lee. You'll believe anything. Don't be such a sucker."

So Tucker had had a stutter in kindergarten, had he? Rainey prodded at her hamburger, trying to decide if a pink interior was a sinister sign. Hadn't she heard it was safer to cook hamburgers all the way through? It was funny that Tucker's stutter should resurface now. She had never heard any evidence of it. She wished now she hadn't mentioned the speech therapy to Ann Lee.

Blake pulled out a chair and sat down. "Where's Tucker?"

Rainey's face burned. Why did Blake have to sit right next to her? There were any number of other places he could have sat. Across the table, for instance, where he wouldn't have been so close.

"Tucker's at speech therapy," Ann Lee supplied.

"Oh, really? What's the problem?"

"I'm not sure he wants everybody to know about it," Rainey said uneasily. "Maybe I shouldn't have mentioned it."

"Heck, I for one think it's great that Tucker is seeking help, finally." Blake reached for the pepper and muttered, "He sure needs it."

Rainey shot Blake a reproachful look. "He never says anything unkind about you."

"Rainey, everybody here knows how I feel about Tucker. I don't see any point in being a hypocrite about it."

Ann Lee and Susan both started talking at once, but then just as suddenly they stopped.

Rainey stood up. "I guess I'm not very hungry." The lump in her throat wouldn't go away.

As she moved off, she heard Blake's plaintive voice behind her, protesting to Ann Lee and Susan, "Don't look at me that way! I didn't say anything! What did I say?"

Rainey could feel blood pushing itself through the blood vessels in her head. She supposed it must be some effect of adrenaline. When she got outside, she stood on the walkway beside the flag, took a deep breath, and listened to the hardware clank against the flagpole. What was bothering her, she realized, was not what Blake had said. She was remembering back when Tucker had been at boarding school in Virginia. She had run into him in the National Museum of Natural History in Washington, D.C. Flags had been flying that day, too, and Tucker had told her that though his school thought he was having a lot of dental work done in the city, the truth was that he came into D.C. and hung around museums to pick up girls.

Dental appointments—speech therapy. It was hard not to notice the parallel. If only she hadn't mentioned the speech therapy at lunch! Blake probably hadn't believed Tucker's story for a minute. He had once warned her that Tucker collected girls.

She looked up and watched the flag flapping in the wind and struggled with herself. Forget Blake, she told herself. The question was simple—did she trust Tucker or not? It was a delicate question. Her mind seemed to be hopelessly confused ever since Blake had got back in town. It was just possible that it wasn't Tucker she distrusted but herself—she had to keep that in mind.

A motorcycle roared around the traffic circle and choked down to a stop. Rainey found herself looking into the smoldering eyes of C. G. Bowman, and she instinctively backed away.

C.G. took off her helmet and squinted into the sun. The gold studs in her ears glittered. "Don't worry. I'm not going to bite you."

"I'm not afraid of you." Rainey lifted her chin defiantly. "Actually, I was hoping to run into you." That was untrue, but Rainey had a feeling it would interest C.G.

C.G. looked interested.

Rainey took a deep breath. Suddenly in a flash it had all become clear to her. All her confusion coalesced and gelled into determination. She felt as if C.G. had been *sent*. Nobody else could be counted on to do what she needed done. "I want you to follow someone for me." She had spoken louder than she intended and immediately she felt embarrassed.

"Follow someone?"

"Like they do on detective shows. I'll pay you."

C.G.'s eyes narrowed. "Who do you want me to follow?"

Rainey's throat felt dry. What was she doing making a deal with C. G. Bowman? She must be out of her mind. "This is strictly confidential, isn't it?"

"I don't make promises." C.G. shrugged.

Rainey hesitated. Realistically speaking, she had no choice. She needed C.G. and she would have to take her as she found her. "Okay, listen. Do you think you could follow somebody's car without being seen?"

"No problem." C.G. gnawed at her thumbnail. "Ten dollars an hour plus expenses."

"I want you to follow Tucker Harbisson. He drives a yellow Mustang with a 'Life Is a Beach' bumper sticker."

"I know the car."

"You'll do it, then?"

"I might. Your case interests me."

Rainey pulled out her wallet and handed C.G. a ten-dollar bill. "I don't want you to hurt him. I mean, I don't want him dead or anything."

"What do you take me for? A hit man?" C.G. examined the bill suspiciously as if she thought it might be counterfeit.

"He has second lunch. Just like us."

"Don't worry. I'll take care of it." C.G. laughed.

C.G., Rainey reflected, was in a class by herself. Offhand, Rainey couldn't think of any other girl who would look natural accessorized with an ammo belt.

As she walked to class, Rainey was pursued by a number of unpleasant second thoughts. What if Tucker found out she had hired C.G. to tail him? How would it look?

It would look as if she didn't trust him, that's how it would look.

Well, all right, she didn't trust him. She had to face that. The ten dollars she had paid C.G. was proof of it.

Maybe her suspicion of him was only her own craziness. Maybe it was all tied up in what she felt about her father or even her feelings about Blake, but there it was—she didn't trust Tucker. She had gone too far now to turn back. She simply couldn't wimp out and run back to tell C.G. she had changed her mind.

"Rainey!" Blake ran to catch up with her.

All at once Rainey had the awful feeling that he had seen her talking to C.G., that he knew all about her putting a tail on Tucker. She was feeling slightly ashamed of herself.

"Still speaking to me?" he asked.

"Sure."

"You aren't mad?"

"No." She groped in her purse for a handkerchief. She

could feel her eyes filling up, and she was afraid the tears might begin to spill over. "Look," she said desperately, "I know that Tucker's got his faults. I mean, nobody's perfect, right? So don't worry about it." She blew her nose. "I understand, really I do, that you wouldn't feel about him the way I felt about him."

"God, I hope not. Wait a minute. Did you say *felt?* Are we talking past tense here?"

It seemed to Rainey that she was in one of those awful dreams where every time she tried to escape she ran bang into something. She was glad she had hired C.G. If she could just get this settled, she was sure everything would start to make sense again.

"Rainey?" Blake yelled.

She had gone on into French class.

Six

The following afternoon when Rainey went out to her car after school, C.G. was leaning against the fender readjusting one of her earrings. She had three earrings in each earlobe, so constant maintenance was necessary.

"I wish you wouldn't lean on the car," Rainey said. "It's old and kind of delicate. What did you find out?"

"He went over to the junior college."

"What? Did you say the junior college?"

"The community college—you know, off State Road Fifty-six. It was kind of tricky following him out there on the highway. I thought this was going to be an in-city job only. You owe me five bucks for expenses and an extra five bucks hazard pay."

"Hazard pay? What are you talking about?"

"That's a truck route, babe. You should see those suckers whiz by."

Rainey reached into her wallet and gave C.G. a five; then she counted out four ones. C.G. waited impatiently as she counted out the remaining four quarters.

"He parked his car by this Student Union sign." C.G. stashed the bills in her hip pocket and sucked on her finger meditatively. "If you want, I could follow him inside the next time and see who he's meeting."

"No. No, I don't want you to do that. It doesn't matter."

C.G.'s dark eyes burned in a way Rainey found vaguely alarming. She resisted looking behind her. "Uh, I appreciate your good work," she said nervously.

"It was fun." C.G. pocketed the change. "In fact, this could be a possible career for me, you know? I kind of see myself as a detective. So this guy is cheating on you, huh? I guess you're pretty mad."

"Not really. I mean, not exactly."

"I kind of thought you were. The way you look all white in the face and all, you know?"

To Rainey's alarm, C.G. seemed to want to stand around and chat. The situation was delicate in the extreme. Rainey was in no mood to spell out the details of her personal life to satisfy C.G.'s curiosity, but she didn't want to get C.G. annoyed. She remembered all too well what had happened when Missy Melinik did that. "Well, thank you very much," she said. She fished her last quarter out of her change purse. "Here's a tip."

"*De nada.*" C.G. sketched a farewell with one hand and slunk off. Rainey supposed that somewhere near the janitor's closet she had a lair or a hideout or something. It was certainly hard to envision her actually going to classes.

The peculiar thing, Rainey thought, as she got into her car, was that she was not staggered by the news about Tucker. Upset, yes. Surprised, no. She had almost seen it coming. She understood it all now—Tucker was hanging out over at the college hoping to run into the blond girl with the dimples. The rat.

Before climbing into her car and driving away, she spent a pleasant moment thinking of how she could pour sugar in his gas tank or hire a hit man to fracture his knee-caps.

The lowest thing about him, she decided, was that he hadn't had the decency to break up with her as soon as he got interested in somebody else. None of that polite fiction of "I think we both ought to start seeing other people." No, he was going to wait until he had Dimples securely hooked before he dumped her.

The fear that consumed Rainey now was that he'd manage to break up with her before she broke up with him.

She spotted a pay phone on the corner near a gas station. At once she pulled her car over, tires squealing, and jumped out. She grubbed in her change purse. Three pennies. Blast! She had given C.G. her last quarter! Grinding her teeth, she got back in her car and drove to work.

"Marty," she said as soon as she walked in the back door of McDonald's. "Would you lend me a quarter? I have to make an important phone call."

"You could use the company phone."

"No, I'd better not."

He smiled. "Oh. That kind of phone call." He handed her the quarter.

Rainey hated to think what kind of phone call Marty had in mind. Did he imagine she was calling her bookie? She ran outside to the public phone, dropped in the quarter, and dialed Tucker's number.

"Hello?"

She gasped in relief. It was Tucker's voice. Thank goodness. She didn't know what she would have done if she had gotten his mother or his sister.

"Tucker, this is Rainey. I know this seems awfully sudden, but I've done a lot of thinking about this, and I think we both ought to start seeing other people."

"What?"

"See other people. S-e-e—"

"I can spell it, Rainey. What is this? It sounds like a truck going by out there. What's going on? Where are you? In the middle of the highway?"

"I'm at a pay phone. I've got to go now. I've got to get to work."

"This is all Blake's doing, isn't it?"

"Blake doesn't have anything to do with it!" Rainey exclaimed.

"Then what's this about 'other people'? Exactly what other people are you talking about?"

He sounded so angry that for an awful moment Rainey wondered if C.G. had got her facts straight. Maybe she had been wrong to trust C.G. But why would C.G. have made up that stuff about the college student union? No, it all made sense. Tucker had been lying to her.

"Rainey, we've got to talk."

She didn't want to give him the satisfaction of knowing that he had forced her hand. She wanted him to think her feelings for him had just fizzled out peacefully. "There's nothing to talk about. No hard feelings, okay?" She had to pause to unclench her teeth. "It's just one of those things. 'Bye."

"Rainey!"

She hung up. She leaned against the phone and spent a pleasant moment imagining that Tucker would marry Dimples and that they would grow grossly fat and disgusting and have six disgusting children who dribbled at the table when small and got in trouble with the law when big. She imagined herself stopping by the convenience store where Tucker and Dimples worked double shifts to support their large brood. "How *lovely* to see you again," she would coo, flinging her fur casually over one shoulder. "Oh, dear, I must run. The alarm seems to be going off in my Ferrari. Someone must be trying to get at my diamond necklace. But let me autograph a copy of my best-selling horror novel for you before I go. It's called *Fried Boyfriends*."

The smell of hamburgers hit her as soon as she went in the back door at work. "I won't tell anybody you got in late," Marty promised her. "Want to take the drive-in window?"

Rainey wished she could go home, throw herself on the bed, and cry, but instead she stoically took her post at the drive-in window.

She went about filling the next order like an automaton. She slapped a lid on the milkshake Marty handed her and put the fries in a white bag. When she slid back the glass window and looked down, to her surprise there was Blake holding a five-dollar bill out the window of the Corvette.

"Are you okay?" He shot a worried look up at her.

"Blake! I didn't recognize your voice when you ordered. Everybody sounds so funny through the speaker." She sniffled. "Just got something in my eye. Do you want extra ketchup?"

"Look, Rainey, do you need to talk or something?"

She blew her nose. "I'm okay. I just broke up with Tucker, that's all."

"I see." He paused. "Well, naturally you're upset."

"I'm not upset!" She handed him the bag of fries. "I'm not a bit upset. I'm mad! There's a big difference. What you see are tears of rage!"

Blake put the paper bags on the seat beside him. "I'm coming back when you get off work, okay?"

She nodded. She leaned out the window and watched him drive off. When she pulled her head back in, she caught her reflection in the window and decided to comb her hair before Blake came back. She was already feeling much better. It might not be necessary to shoot Tucker in the kneecaps, after all.

"So she paid me to follow him and he went out to the college to the student union." C.G. was sitting on Michael's lap playing with his gray hair. "I'll bet nobody ever asks you for your I.D.," she said wistfully.

"Come on, C.G., you know me. I stick to raspberry tea."

"Don't you ever do anything that's bad for you?"

He grinned. "Well, I go out with you."

"Hey, I'm the best thing that ever happened to you. Who taught you all you know about carburetors?"

He frowned. "I still don't get this stuff about Tucker and the student union. Why would Rainey care if he goes out there?"

"Use your head, Mikey. He has another girl, obviously."

"You think?"

"Sure. She turned white as an egg when I told her. Believe me, the girl was shook."

"I wonder if this means it's over between them."

"What do you care? Have you got a thing about her or something?"

"No, but I know somebody who does."

C.G. pressed her lips against Michael's.

"Mmmm," he said.

"Better than raspberry tea?" she asked finally.

When Rainey left work that evening, Blake was waiting in the parking lot.

She slid into the seat beside him.

"Tell me all about it."

"There's not much to say. It's just fizzled out. Actually—" She hesitated. She hated to tell Blake an outright lie. "Actually, it's not exactly true that it fizzled out. It turned out he wasn't going to speech therapy after all. He was going over to the student union at the junior college."

"Why would he do that?"

"To pick up girls, I guess." She shrugged.

"But how did you find out?"

"I paid C.G. to tail him."

"You didn't!" he whooped.

69

"I really appreciate your not saying 'I told you so.' I know you must be thinking it, but—"

"Jeez, every time I think of C.G. roaring along behind him! She must have looked like an angel of doom. I'll bet he was sweating blood."

"It wouldn't be like that at all! Naturally, she would try to be discreet."

"C.G. discreet! I love it!"

"Don't tell anybody, okay, Blake? My story is going to be that it just—"

"Fizzled out."

"Right."

"Have you had supper?" He looked at her. "Maybe you don't have any appetite."

"Actually, I'm starving." Rainey realized that she really was hungry. "Let's get something to eat. Anything but hamburgers. I don't ever want to see another hamburger."

They went to a Chinese restaurant. The waitress led them to a back booth and then minced away. "So how does it feel to be a free agent again?" Blake asked.

"It feels—well, funny."

He looked disappointed. "The correct answer is 'It feels great! Boy, am I glad to get rid of that jerk!' Got it?"

"I'll work on it." She smiled a little. "Sometimes you sound like Michael."

"I'm not like Michael. You know that. I'm cautious, conventional, respectable, and all those dull things."

"You don't have to sound depressed about it. I like you just the way you are."

He grabbed both her hands. "Do you really?"

Rainey felt a sudden surge of sick panic.

"Did I say something wrong?" Blake asked, alarmed.

"I think I'm getting a headache or something."

"Let's ask the waitress if she can dig up an aspirin somewhere."

"I—I think I saw some by the cash register. I'll be right back."

Rainey fled. She had to wait until the person ahead of her paid his check, which was good because it gave her a chance to calm down. When she got to the cash register she bought a packet of aspirin and went to the ladies' room. She put an aspirin in her mouth, bent over to drink water out of the faucet, then wiped her hand across her mouth. Oriental dragons made of dark wood were coiled around the mirror framing her image—her pale face and alarmed dark eyes.

She liked Blake very much, more than she liked anyone else in the world, probably. They understood each other. And when he pulled up at that drive-in window, she had never been so glad to see anybody in her life. But now she had this crazy impulse to run out of the restaurant. What was the matter with her? Did she imagine that everyone who loved her would end up leaving her?

When she got back to the table, two small bowls of egg drop soup had been served.

"You okay?" Blake asked anxiously.

"Sure. I'm fine." She spread a napkin on her lap.

"Rainey, you remember the time you told me that you thought Susan was in love with me?"

"Scared you out of your mind, didn't I?"

"You aren't feeling that way, are you?"

She blinked. "No! No, of course not."

71

"Good," he said. "Because that would have been tough for me to handle. Look, you've had a long day, I've had a long day. Why don't we just get something to eat, and we'll talk about—oh, chemistry or something." He caught himself. "No, no, I didn't mean chemistry, exactly. Just let's talk about something dull and everyday and boring. Okay?"

She stirred her soup with her spoon, then tentatively smiled at him. "Okay."

SEVEN

Thursday afternoon rain poured outside Michael's bedroom window and streamed in sheets down the panes. The glow of a lamp illuminated his *Casablanca* poster. Books and magazines spilled off the bed and over onto the floor, and his large collection of VCR cassettes stood on end all along the baseboards like oversize dominoes waiting to be set in motion. A denim jacket hung precariously on the bedpost.

Michael, straddling his desk chair, watched Blake pace the floor. He decided he wouldn't care to change places with Blake even if he threw in the Corvette. Blake was too high-strung. To be him for a week could tire a guy out.

Blake rattled the keys in his pocket. "I just don't want to make the wrong move, that's all."

"She's dumped Tucker, man. What's the problem?"

"Okay, you might say that technically she's dumped Tucker, but the fact is he was the one who was fooling around, so it's more like he dumped her. Do you follow me? I mean, I have the feeling—oh, heck, I don't know what feeling I've got."

"You're going nuts, that's what. The pale, fevered brow, the trembling hands. You need to ask yourself—what do doctors recommend most often for acid indigestion?"

"Sure, sure."

"I'm only trying to help. Believe me, man, you think too much. A guy and a girl—what's to think about? It's all basic, primitive. It's instinct."

"You've been hanging around with C.G. too much. Now all of a sudden everything's instinct. Coincidence?" Blake lifted his brows. "Nah!"

"I like that! Do I stand here and mock your tenderest feelings?"

"Okay, I'm sorry. I apologize." Blake sat down on the bed. "Just as a matter of curiosity, what do your parents think of C.G.?"

"She's not the kind of girl you take home to Mom and Dad, of course."

"I'll say!"

"But I've done a lot of talking about her and I have the definite impression that they are pleased I'm going out with a girl my own age." Michael beamed. "As soon as she gets herself a dress, I might just bring her by here for a quick hello. Dad's been having a lot of trouble with his alternator. She might be able to help him out." He held up his hand. "But I wouldn't want you to think I only love C.G. because she helps keep my bike running."

"No?"

"No, man. I mean, the warmth, the passion!"

"I seem to remember you've mentioned that a time or two."

Michael grinned. "I like living on the edge. 'Born to be wi-ild,' " he warbled. "Speaking of which, you'd better shove off. I've got to shower for my hot date."

"C.G. and you going to roast marshmallows over the engine block?"

Michael pitched a dog-eared copy of *Rolling Stone* at him.

When it was time for Michael to pick up C.G., it was drizzling steadily, so he borrowed his dad's car instead of taking his bike. On the way over to C.G.'s apartment he whistled tunelessly.

Her apartment was upstairs in a large complex. C.G. came to the door in a tight denim skirt and a filmy shirt that set Michael's blood pounding in his ears. Her mouth was a scarlet slash on her white face, and her dark eyes looked like two coals. She had the kind of neat little nose that cartoonists depict with a short curved line.

"You won't be late, will you?" asked Mrs. Bowman. "This is a school night, remember."

"No problem, Mrs. B. We're just going to get the early-bird special at the steak house, take a quick, uh, drive around town maybe, and we'll be back in plenty of time to do homework, right, C.G.?"

" 'Bye," C.G. said flatly.

As they walked downstairs, Michael pursed his lips and whistled appreciatively.

"You like the outfit, huh?"

"I like *you*, girl, va-voom!" He scooped her up in his arms and carried her to the car. To him she seemed like a sweet-smelling little thing, but he felt vaguely sorry for her mother. He sensed it wouldn't be easy to be C.G.'s mother.

The sidewalks were shiny, and when they reached the car he could see that beads of rain had collected on the windshield catching the pink light of the early evening.

When they got into the car, C.G. pressed herself close to his side. She kept her hand on his knee as they drove to the steak house, and Michael found his breath coming quickly. He parked the car in back of the restaurant by the Dumpster and reached for her. She laughed at him, showing a flash of white teeth.

"Who needs food?" he muttered.

"All living beings," she retorted. "Including me."

"Sheesh." He threw her door open. "All right—steak and baked potato coming up."

He stood watching as C.G. circled the car, then grabbed her hand as she reached him. "C.G., tell me something—are you happy?"

"That's a weird question."

"Rate your happiness on a scale of one to ten. People do it all the time on polls."

"I don't think that way, Mikey. I don't think happy-unhappy."

"Liar."

"Okay, I'm not happy. Satisfied?"

"You don't have to get mad about it."

"Let's get something to eat."

The early-bird special was patronized heavily by families.

Booster chairs were much in evidence, along with balloons tied to the backs of chairs.

Michael and C.G. took a booth by the big windows facing the street. It was gloomy outside and rain dripped down the window. A strong aroma of steak filled the brightly lit dining area. Stacks of plastic dishes could be heard colliding in the kitchen. C.G. looked around the room without much interest and toyed with her baked potato.

A toddler broke loose from her family's table and tottered past them. She wore a pink barrette, and her lips were sticky with peppermint candy. Her amused father followed close behind. "Whoa! Come on, Cindy." He scooped her up and bore her off.

"I used to be happy when I was little like that," said C.G. suddenly.

"Me, too. Jeez, age two! The peak of human existence. Splish-splashing in the bathtub with your rubber ducky, nice security blanky, snacktime every time you turn around, and a warm thumb to suck on at bedtime. Maybe we should have stopped there while we were ahead."

"Yeah."

Michael was sorry he had even brought up the happiness-unhappiness thing. There was a bereft look in C.G.'s eyes that he hated to think he was responsible for.

He cut into his steak and changed the subject. "Blake was over at my house just now driving himself crazy about Rainey."

"Oh, yeah?"

"Yeah, she's dumped Tucker and she's going out with him. What more does he want, for pity's sake?"

"Maybe he wants to be sure she really likes him. Maybe he thinks she's just using him."

"Whaa? Why would he think something like that?" Michael stared.

She sucked up iced tea in her straw, then held it in the straw by sealing the top with her finger. "See, the tea won't run out because nature abhors a vacuum."

"Very interesting. What's the matter, C.G.? Is something bothering you? Out with it."

"Maybe I just want to be two years old again."

"Well, I don't want you to be two years old, and I have to tell you there would be quite a few technical difficulties to work out if you tried it."

"Yeah. I'd have to get all new clothes." She smiled.

Later, as they were driving home, the rain stopped, but Michael could hear the water rushing in the gutters. "I guess we're kind of later than I thought getting home. Is your mother going to be mad?"

"I don't care if she's mad or not. Actually, I might run away."

Michael frowned. "What kind of thing is that to say?"

"Would you miss me?"

"Well, sure I'd miss you, but it's just a dumb thing to say! Really big-time stupid. You've only got a year more of school and then you'll be leaving anyway, so what's this stuff about running away? It's dumb."

"You aren't in my skin!" C.G. shouted. "You don't know what it's like to be me!"

"Look, you don't have to yell at me! What do you expect me to say? 'Running away is a great idea—let me pack your bags'? Don't talk like an idiot."

As they turned onto the bridge, the Chevy's headlights momentarily illuminated leafy branches sticking up out of the swollen water. It had been a year of heavy rainfall and the river had risen high enough on the banks to swamp some low-lying trees.

"Maybe I am an idiot," she said sullenly.

Michael reached for her, but she wiggled out of his reach and kicked her door open.

He slammed on the brakes. "You want to wreck the car?" he yelled. "That door can tear right off, you know."

She slid out of the car, slammed the door behind her, and disappeared into the darkness.

Michael swore. Glancing behind him swiftly, he switched on the blinker lights and jumped out of the car. "C.G.?" he yelled. "Get back in the car, for Pete's sake. Where are you?" The headlights of the car shone straight ahead on the deserted bridge, and the wind sighed in the tree branches on the banks. Michael ran to the cement and metal railing and looked down at the swollen black water. "C.G.!" he screamed. He looked around frantically, but saw no sign of her. The headlights and a streetlight high overhead gave just enough illumination for him to see that the street going over the bridge was deserted. His stomach squeezed sickeningly as he looked down at the river. If she had gone in, it was all finished. He would never find her in that water. At the thought of C.G. in the black river, being swept farther away every second, he impulsively stepped over the railing. He hesitated on the cement escarpment, a parade of images flashing before his eyes. Desperate, scarcely knowing what he was doing, he pulled off his shoes and threw them over the railing behind him.

"Surprise!" shrieked C.G. She had jumped out from the shadows cast by his headlights shining against the cement base of the railing.

Michael gripped the railing tight as he tried to catch his breath and stay on his feet. He was so shaken he was afraid he might go over into the water if he wasn't careful. His vision blurred.

"Did you think I'd gone over?"

"Yeah." Michael took a deep breath and scrambled back over the railing. There was a roaring in his mind that drowned out thought. He found one shoe by the car's rear wheel. He put it on and hobbled around until he found the other one.

"Were you really going in after me?" asked C.G. "Is that why you took your shoes off?"

"Get in the car, C.G."

"Are you mad?"

"Get in the car!" Michael yelled.

When he got behind the wheel, C.G. seemed subdued. "Aren't you going to say anything?" she said in a small voice.

Michael didn't trust himself to speak. He was afraid of what he might say. The last thing he wanted was for C.G. to jump out of the car and throw herself under the wheels, and he was beginning to think she was perfectly capable of doing that. So he drove in silence, so angry that his eyes were hot, so angry that his head felt swollen, so angry he could have killed her. Driving with exaggerated care at five miles below the posted speed limit, he pulled into the parking lot of West Mount Apartments.

"Come on, Mikey. Can't you take a joke?"

He reached over and threw her door open in a jerky movement. "Life and death is not a joking matter. Call me old-fashioned, but that's the way I see it."

When she reached for him he brushed her hand away.

"Goodbye," he said formally. "And good luck with your next victim."

She choked on a sob. "Mikey!"

"I can't take this, C.G. I'm sorry, but that's the way it is. This is it. Goodbye, and I mean it."

She hesitated, and Michael wondered if he was going to have to shove her out of the car. The way he felt, it would have been a pleasure not only to push her out but to throw her against the pavement. Finally, to his infinite relief, she got out.

He reached over and slammed the door closed. It might have been the wind, but he almost thought he heard her calling after him as he drove away. He felt as if he wanted to drive so far away he could never hear her voice again. He felt like digging a moat around his house, building a drawbridge, and getting an unlisted number. His flesh was still cold from the shock of what had happened on the bridge. He'd never forget it; he'd never get away from it. He felt sick.

When he thought he could talk about it without shaking all over, he drove over to Blake's house.

Mrs. Farraby's eye surveyed him through the peephole in the front door. "Michael! Is anything wrong? Dr. Farraby is still at the hospital." She opened the door and looked at him anxiously.

"I just want to talk to Blake."

"I think he said he was going to go to bed early." She blinked at him. "Is it anything I can help you with?"

"I just need to talk to Blake for a little while. It won't take long." He strode past her, went on upstairs, and opened the door to Blake's room.

Blake sat up suddenly in the bed. A fat paperback called *Preparing for the SATs* slid to the floor. "What's wrong?"

Michael closed the door and sat down heavily. "C.G. and I split up."

"What happened?"

Michael told him.

"Jeez, were you really going in after her?"

Michael shook his head. "It would have been suicide. How could I? I mean, I hardly even knew what I was doing. I was falling apart, you know? But I got this flash in my mind—of my parents finding that empty car on the bridge. And, man, I knew I couldn't go in after her."

"She's crazy, doing something like that. She's got to be."

"I'm never going to forget it." His voice was bitter. "I'm always going to know I'm the kind of guy who would let his girl be drowned and not even get his feet wet."

"But look here, it would have been insane to go in. You said that yourself. It would have been suicide. And as it turned out she wasn't in the river anyway."

"Right. But I still feel like slime. And the thing that gets me is that she did this to me just for kicks."

"Just put it out of your mind, man. It's history. Put it behind you."

"Yeah, well, it reminds me of those immortal words"—his mouth twisted—"'Never eat at a place called Mom's, never play cards with a man called Doc, and never go out with a girl who has bigger troubles than you do.'" Michael stood up. "I think it was Anonymous who said that. Very prolific writer, Anonymous."

"Well, for what it's worth, I think you're doing the right thing, breaking it off."

"I don't have any choice, chum. I swear, if I touched her, my fingers would curl right around her throat." He hesitated, his hand on the doorknob. "Look, I'm not going to tell anybody else about this."

"Sure. Fine."

"I just don't want to go into it. The whole thing makes me sick to my stomach. I'll probably never be able to go over that bridge again. Go over that bridge? Heck, I'll probably never be able to sleep again."

"You'll feel better tomorrow, I'll bet. Get some sleep."

"Yeah. Easy to say."

Michael closed the door behind him.

EIGHT

"Michael has broken up with C.G.," Susan told Ann Lee as they went into homeroom.

"Are you sure?"

"Bitsy Ferguson told me. She saw that Michael looked kind of down when he got out of his car this morning. So she gave him a ten-page questionnaire and a lie detector test and held him up by his heels and shook all his secrets out of him—or something. You know the way she is."

"Gee! I wonder if this means they've broken up for good."

"But definitely. Absolutely. Michael told her he was considering having a moat dug around his house."

"That does sound definite."

The girls sat down in adjoining desks. Outside the classroom windows, the sun was shining through dark clouds, giving the grass a fragile quicksilver brilliance. Mrs. Ansley called roll, then methodically began working her way through the announcements. Finally she said, "As you all know, the homecoming queen and her court are to be elected soon. With this in mind, the Student Council has sent all classes a memorandum about how we might make the event more meaningful."

"Let's nominate Mrs. Ansley!" someone called.

"No! Bill the Cat!"

Mrs. Ansley froze them with a look. "The nominations will be submitted only by recognized school organizations, as usual, but the Student Council would like all of you who are members of these organizations to consider giving this recognition to someone who has made a real contribution to West Mount High, a contribution of both her time and her talent."

"Yeah, boy," sneered a kid at the back. "I'm telling you, Bill the Cat is just another pretty face!"

"*Just* a thought," Mrs. Ansley went on frigidly. "This is your high school, people, and if you want homecoming to be a joke or a popularity contest, well, it's up to you."

"I nominate Mother Teresa!" someone cried.

The bell rang.

"I'll bet you'll be homecoming queen, Susan." Ann Lee immediately wished she had kept quiet. It seemed to be a reflex, her acting as Susan's admiring chorus.

"Shhh. Don't even say it. It's bad luck." Susan's heart-shaped face was flushed with a faint color and she looked every inch the homecoming queen receiving the homage of her subjects. She was wearing a soft brown wraparound blouse that exposed her shoulders and a skirt of filmy cotton embellished with expensive scrolls of embroidery. Her nails were enameled brown to match her blouse, and the heavy bangles on her wrists looked as if they had been stripped from the body of a Gypsy princess. You had to give it to her—she understood clothes.

She edged her way with many smiles through the crunch at the classroom door, then turned to Ann Lee as they stepped out into the hall. "You want to hear something crazy? You know, when you went off this summer, I got myself all worked up into this state worrying about how you would have changed. Isn't that funny?" She grinned. "Friends forever, right?"

Ann Lee managed to smile weakly. "Right." She trotted a bit to keep up. "So, is Michael real upset about this breakup with C.G., or what?"

"I don't know. Bitsy's pretty good on getting her facts straight, but she's not too hot on the fine points of feelings. She did say that he's still wearing his earring."

"Something to remember her by?"

"Dunno. Maybe he just likes the earring. I knew those two couldn't last. I mean, it was, like, truly *bizarre!* Sort of a case of Godzilla meets Rambo."

"Michael's not a bit like Godzilla."

"Well, of course not. Not *literally*. But he's not exactly your average person, either. You have to admit that." Susan flashed a brilliant smile and lifted her hand in farewell as she went into her class. She might have been practicing a gracious greeting to the crowd in the football stadium.

Her head down, Ann Lee moved on along the hall. So Susan was relieved she hadn't changed. But she *had* changed. She had! The trouble was, she needed some outward sign of it to make people notice. She needed doves swooping down from the sky carrying a banner: "See the new Ann Lee!" Or a different hair color, at least. Except that her mother would have a stroke if she changed her hair color.

Not breaking her stride, Ann Lee sidestepped a huge football player and moved out of the path of a flying wedge of sophomores who were chewing candy bars with open mouths to see who would be grossed out first. Years of navigating the halls of West Mount had made the moves second nature. She stepped over somebody's spilled books, then swiftly pressed herself against the wall to avoid being run down by C. G. Bowman. Unseeing, C.G. charged past her, fists clenched and eyes blazing. Anybody who had even rudimentary survival skills would be getting out of C.G.'s way today.

A few minutes later when Ann Lee took her seat in physics class she was hit suddenly by a fascinating thought. Now that Michael and C.G. had broken up, why shouldn't she be Michael's next love interest?

She could think of a number of reasons, actually, beginning with her vaguely pear-shaped figure and winding up with her fear of motorcycles, but she refused to dwell on these difficulties. She should give it a try. She had changed. This could be the proof of it.

Ann Lee had never actually tried to get a boy interested in her before. She had had her hopes, of course—beautiful pastel dreams, sort of like hand lotion ads—but she hadn't taken any actual steps to achieve her goal. It was very possible that this had been her trouble all along. After all, far more unattractive girls than she had boyfriends. She had to look at it this way—if C.G. could have a boyfriend, anybody could.

At lunch Ann Lee spotted Blake and Rainey sitting together. It was a little tactless, perhaps, to butt in at their table. Now that Rainey and Tucker had broken up and Blake at last had a clear field, Ann Lee knew he wouldn't welcome her presence. But if she wanted to see Michael, she had to go where he'd be. And since he had broken up with C.G., he'd probably sit with Blake.

"Hi! Okay if I sit with you two?"

Blake looked startled. "Sure." He pulled a chair out for her. Ann Lee's plate rattled as she put her tray down. Her nerves were pretty frayed, she realized.

"So." She put her napkin in her lap and groped wildly for some topic of conversation far removed from Michael. "I guess Susan's going to be homecoming queen, huh?"

Blake blew into his straw and the paper wrapping flew off. "Oh, yeah, they were talking about that in homeroom this morning, weren't they?"

"Susan hasn't done that much public service work, though," Rainey pointed out. "She's popular, but you can't think of anything she's actually done for the school."

"You really think anybody pays attention to the stuff the Student Council says?" Blake asked. "Think of it this way—who was homecoming queen last year?"

"Melanie Martin."

He grinned. "I rest my case."

Ann Lee wanted to ask Blake what he knew about the breakup between Michael and C.G., but she was afraid that if she did, her personal interest in the question would be too glaringly obvious. She cleared her throat. "So, don't let me interrupt anything, you guys. What were you talking about?''

They glanced at each other, and Ann Lee belatedly realized that they might have been talking about something quite personal.

"We were talking about life," Rainey said at last.

"In a general sort of way," Blake added.

"Like, for example, Blake is religious."

"Well, I was brought up that way," he said apologetically.

"But I'm not. I figure you have to go into life and get what you want out of it." Rainey cut into her meat loaf impatiently. "Life is like a pretzel. You have to bend it to the shape you want."

"I sort of see what you mean." Ann Lee cautiously put her hand out for the salt shaker, keeping her eyes on Rainey. "I kind of think you have to go after what you want, too. I've been thinking that a lot lately."

"The thing is you can't just"—Rainey made a helpless gesture with her fork—"feel your way. If you do that, your life spins out in some crazy way you never planned and you get swept along with it. You have to plan, to work toward your goals."

"Sounds pretty depressing," commented Blake. "Actually, it sounds a lot like my father."

"But there has to be a place in life for feelings," Ann Lee put in timidly.

"Well, yes." Rainey stared doubtfully at her forkful of mashed potatoes as if she couldn't remember how it had gotten into her hand. "But the trouble with feelings is that you can't count on them. They come and go."

"Some feelings you can count on." Blake grinned crookedly. "Hey, my parents have been married for twenty-five years. That's a quarter of a century, folks."

Ann Lee looked from one to the other in confusion. She wasn't sure anymore what they were talking about. Love? Commitment? Getting involved? Grade-point averages? Maybe they weren't sure, either. Maybe the meaning was all between the lines. But it sounded touchy, and she wasn't about to ask. It sounded almost as if Rainey was trying to fend Blake off, and that didn't make any sense. Why would she want to do that?

Michael let his tray fall on the table with a sound like an explosion. "Death to traitors!"

Blake gave a short laugh. "Boy, everybody around here's a ray of sunshine."

"Don't look at me, man. I'm happy. Can't you see it in my eyes? I mean, if you get past their faintly bloodshot quality." Michael pulled his bottom eyelids down to show the red lining, and Ann Lee hastily looked away. "I'm chairman of the homecoming float committee, folks. Does earth hold greater glory?"

"How'd you get sucked into that?"

"Sherry Parker got a hangnail and said she couldn't handle it. What could I do? You can count on me, I said. I'll step into the breach. Or is it broach? Anyway, that's the line where the trumpets always sound offscreen, so it doesn't much matter which." Michael dispatched his meatloaf, then attacked his roll. He made fast progress. His method was simple—his cheeks bulged briefly, he swallowed, and the food was gone. He eyed Blake's plate hungrily. "If you don't want that roll, I'll take it off your hands."

Blake put both hands protectively over his food. "I want it. I want it. Down, boy. Get away."

"You can have mine." Ann Lee lifted her roll in a napkin and put it on Michael's plate.

"Hey, you sure?" He didn't wait for an answer but downed it at once and washed it down with a healthy swig of chocolate milk. He burped. "The food around here is disgusting."

"How do you know?" said Blake. "It goes down so fast I don't see how you even taste it."

"I try not to, of course, but I do taste it. You've heard of speed readers? I'm a speed eater. We speed eaters get every nuance of flavor in half the time."

Ann Lee chuckled.

Michael looked at her. "I didn't think it was that good, but don't stop laughing on account of me."

"Would you like some of my meatloaf?" she offered. "I'm not very hungry."

"If you insist." He neatly cut away a third of the slab of meatloaf and transferred it to his plate. "My life is ashes, but I have to keep going somehow. Calories seem to be the answer. Short-term, anyway."

"So, do you need help on that float committee?" Ann Lee asked.

"I thought you were already handling the advertisements in the program."

"Well, I am," she admitted. "But I'm always willing to put in a little extra time for a good cause."

"Sure. Peons are always welcome. Any other volunteers? Don't everybody talk at once, now. Come on, come on.

Jeez, the public spirit at this table is very low. I'm surprised at you people.''

"Don't look at me," said Rainey. "I have to work."

"But, Blake, you're going to be at homecoming, aren't you? They always need convertibles for the homecoming court to ride in, right? You need to do your bit. And you don't want to be associated with something second class, do you? We need to get working on this thing. It's a big event."

"Not me. I'm not contributing the 'Vette. Count me out."

"I see your point." Michael squashed his empty chocolate milk carton with his fist. "What's the fun in having all those pretty girls draped all over you? Who needs it?"

"Sitting on my car, you mean. Scuffing it, maybe even scratching it with their dumb bracelets? Don't talk to me about it."

"The man has thought deeply and profoundly on this subject. I bow to greater wisdom."

After lunch Ann Lee made an attempt to walk with Michael, but he didn't seem to realize that she was trying to keep up with him and he got ahead of her. A fight had broken out in the boys' restroom on A wing, and they got separated by the crowd of eager spectators that surged to that end of the building. Finally she shrugged and gave up trying to get through. Her effort to attract Michael's attention had not—so far, she was forced to admit—been a smashing success.

Blake and Michael had managed to get through the crush. They converged at the locker alcove in A wing. "What was that fight about?" asked Blake.

"Dunno. They never seem to be about anything." Michael burped.

"You eat too fast; you better watch it. A guy could choke that way."

"It's my personal home remedy for heartburn." Michael thumped his chest. "Stuffing food in the mouth. Don't laugh. It works."

"You know you'd be crazy to get back with C.G. I don't have to tell you that, do I?"

"Not to worry. I'd just as soon shoot myself in the foot. It's just been sort of a shock, you know? It's kind of been a while since I've been by my lonesome. I may have to put an ad in the paper or something."

"Well, Ann Lee is interested." Blake pulled his English book out of his locker.

"Very funny."

"You didn't notice how she kept shoving food at you and laughing at your crummy jokes?"

"What do you mean, my *crummy* jokes?" Michael drew himself up to his full height. "Anyway, she's just being friendly. Ann Lee and I have been buddies since we were in Pampers."

Blake slammed his locker shut. "Suit yourself."

Later, as he walked to class, Michael found himself thinking about what Blake had said. Ann Lee? He certainly had never thought of Ann Lee as a girl. Of course, she *was* a girl, but he had never had any personal interest in that. But what he found himself struck by at this point was how incredibly different she was from C.G. That was like a recommendation all by itself. Yeah, it was an idea worth thinking about.

NINE

Susan!'' Ann Lee squealed into the phone. ''Michael is coming by any minute to take me to dinner.''

''Michael? Michael Dessaseaux? You're kidding.''

''No, it's true. We were stuffing tissue into chicken wire for the float this afternoon, you know—''

''Get to the good stuff, Ann Lee.''

''Well, anyway, we were just kidding around. You know the way Michael is. Not too many people showed up, and we had a lot of work to do. And all of a sudden he says to me, 'My God, you've got gorgeous eyes, you toothsome wench. How'd you like to go get some tacos with me after we finish this junk?' And I said I wanted to go home and change, and he said he'd pick me up at the house in a few minutes and—eek, he's here, Susan! I hear his bike outside!''

"Well, don't freak out. It's just Michael."

Ann Lee dropped the phone back on the hook and ran to the stairs. This might be "just Michael" to Susan, but to her it was the first genuine, as opposed to arranged-by-others, date she had ever had!

Her mother was walking slowly upstairs with a stunned expression.

"Is that Michael at the door?" Ann Lee asked eagerly.

"He's wearing an earring," her mother said in a funereal tone.

"Cute, isn't it?" Ann Lee checked her appearance in the hall mirror, gave her hair a quick final pat, then charged toward the stairs.

Mrs. Smith caught her hand. "He's on a motorcycle."

"I'm sure he brought an extra helmet." Ann Lee's pulse was racing. She hoped she didn't show how nervous she was. Somehow she had to get past her mother. "Mom, you know Michael. Michael Dessaseaux. He's been in my class for years."

"Millie's son?" Her mother frowned. "The last time I saw him he had just won the prize for finding the most eggs at the Easter egg hunt. He was much, much smaller then."

"Oh, Mom, you've seen him since then. What about in the class play in the seventh grade? He was George Washington."

"This fellow is huge. Gargantuan! Are you sure this is Michael Dessaseaux?"

Ann Lee pecked her mother hastily on the cheek. " 'Bye, Mom. I'm not sure when I'll be back." She raced downstairs before her mother could stop her.

Michael was in the driveway revving up the bike. "Have you ever ridden on one of these things before?" he shouted.

Ann Lee shook her head.

"Nothing to it. Just hold on to me and keep your legs away from the exhaust pipes. They get pretty hot."

Ann Lee scrambled up onto the bike at once. As afraid as she was of the motorcycle, she was more afraid that her mother was going to run out the door to stop her. She took the helmet Michael handed her and strapped it on. Peering apprehensively through its amber wind visor, she noticed that the grass and the trees looked greener, as if she were entering the land of Oz. The bike vibrated under her so that her whole body trembled. She clasped her hands around Michael and breathed a silent prayer.

"Hold on," he warned. "Here we go."

Ann Lee screwed her eyes closed as the bike wheeled into a semicircle, then sped down Hollyberry Lane. The roar was deafening, and the wind beat against her until her legs felt numb. She tried to remind herself of how much she had wanted to have a boyfriend. Did she want one enough to ride a motorcycle? She wasn't sure.

A horn blew behind them and Ann Lee's eyes flew open. Cars whizzed past, missing them by inches. She went cold with fear. Didn't those drivers realize she was completely out in the open on the back of this motorcycle? Being on the back of the bike was worse than being on a traffic island, and she had always loathed traffic islands. This was like being on a traffic island that was speeding insanely.

Michael looked over his shoulder at her. "We're almost there," he yelled.

She wished he would keep his eyes on the road.

A minute later they pulled into the parking lot of Taco Bell, and Michael stripped off his helmet. "How'd you like it?" He turned and beamed at her.

She swallowed and nodded. Her tongue felt glued to the roof of her mouth. She must remember to keep her mouth closed on the ride home. She supposed it had gotten all dried out while she was gasping in terror. She slid to the ground, her knees weak. With a sickening thud she realized that she was going to have to get on the bike again after she ate. Perhaps she had better just nibble very, very cautiously. Her stomach already felt peculiar and she had the feeling it would be unwise to fill it.

Inside, the taco restaurant was warm and crowded. "Eh! Michael!" someone called.

Michael grinned and waved. He nudged Ann Lee gently forward. "We better get in line. It's pretty busy tonight."

When they got up to the counter, Ann Lee ordered a beef taco and a cola.

"Is that all?" said Michael incredulously. "You're going to starve to death. A hummingbird couldn't live on one taco."

"I'm not very hungry. Uh," she said, "I've got to go comb my hair."

Michael smoothed her hair and smiled down at her. "Looks fine to me."

Ann Lee flushed with pleasure. "I'll be right back." She fled to the ladies' room.

"Ann Lee!" Bitsy Ferguson turned away from the mirror in the ladies' room and blotted her lipstick. "Was that Michael I saw you with just now?"

Ann Lee nodded. A brief look in the mirror had confirmed her suspicions. Her hair was a mess. She gave it a few swipes with her comb.

"Tell me, are you the reason he dumped C.G.?" Bitsy's eyes glittered.

Ann Lee hated the way Bitsy was so nosy. She tried to back away, but the room was small. Her shoulderblades pressed against the tile wall. "No, certainly not," she said faintly.

"Well, he didn't waste any time getting back in circulation, did he?"

Ann Lee managed to smile while at the same time shrugging noncommittally. She was already reaching for the doorknob.

"Math Club is putting your name up for homecoming queen," Bitsy said. "I just came from the meeting. I thought you'd want to know."

"It's nice of you to let me know, Bitsy. I'm really honored."

"The names have to be turned in tomorrow, so you'd find out pretty soon anyway." There was a tinge of regret in Bitsy's voice. She evidently preferred to deal in exclusives. "I guess Michael will be your escort, right?"

"I really can't say. Uh, see you!"

Ann Lee found Michael at a small table near a window. "They make these seats so little," he complained, stretching out one leg. "Here. I got you extra hot sauce."

"I just ran into Bitsy Ferguson." Ann Lee sat down. "She says Math Club is putting me up for homecoming queen."

"And you are shocked, flattered, honored, and scarcely know what to say, right?"

"Well, no. I sort of figured"— Ann Lee picked up her taco—"but, anyway—" She stumbled incoherently to a stop. Too much was happening to her all at once. She was finding it hard to process.

"Hey, Michael!" Bitsy simpered at them from across the room.

Michael muttered, "I hate to say a single word to Bitsy. I feel as if I'm being televised live."

"It just makes her feel important to know what's going on, that's all."

Michael quickly dispatched his first taco. "So," he said, "do you have somebody lined up to take you to homecoming?"

"I just found out about being nominated. So naturally, no, I don't have anybody lined up yet."

"I'll go with you, if you'd like."

"I'd like." Ann Lee could feel happiness swelling inside her. She knew Michael would never have offered to escort her to homecoming if he figured their trip to Taco Bell would be their first and last date. It just might be that she had found herself a boyfriend.

When Ann Lee got home, her mother was pacing the floor. "I didn't have a minute's peace the entire time you were gone. I called the Highway Patrol and they said there hadn't been any motorcycle accidents in town this evening. But then I started thinking, what if you were run off the road by a truck and both of you were lying injured in a ditch somewhere, where no one could see you?" She threw her arms around Ann Lee.

"I'm fine, Mom! We weren't even gone very long." Ann Lee detached her mother's arms.

"Those motorcycles are not safe. I wish I had made it outside in time to stop you from going off on that thing. If you're going to date somebody, what's wrong with Blake Farraby? He's a perfectly wonderful boy. I love his parents, and I wouldn't worry about you for a minute if you went someplace with him."

"He hasn't asked me, Mom."

"I might just drop a word to his mother. She told me he hasn't been dating anybody in particular."

"Mom, do *not* speak to his mother." Ann Lee fixed her mother with a fierce glare.

"I don't see why not. If you don't want me to do that, maybe you could make a little effort yourself to attract his interest, Ann Lee. If you would just put yourself out some— you don't have to date dregs, darling, these boys with tattoos and earrings and motorcycles. You don't need that."

"I like Michael, Mom. And he does not have a tattoo."

"Not *yet*," her mother said dolefully.

"He's going to take me to homecoming. Bitsy says I've been nominated." Ann Lee's legs were feeling steadier now. She thought she might be able to make it upstairs after all.

"Nominated for the homecoming court? How nice! We must see about getting a new dress for you—but sweetheart, why do you have to go with Michael? You can't ride in the parade all dressed up on a motorcycle. You must see that."

"I guess we'll use a car then."

Her mother followed her up the stairs. "Ah! So he does have access to a car. Then I don't see why you can't ride in a car whenever you go out together. In fact, I expect your father will insist upon it." She froze suddenly. "On the other hand, I'm not sure I want you in a car with that boy."

"Oh, Mom!"

"I know you're going to say I shouldn't be so concerned about appearances, but like it or not, the way people look sends a message about them. What kind of message does Michael send? A lack of respect for authority, a disdain for what other people think, a flagrant disregard for the standards of the community—that's the message he sends."

"I've got to do my homework, Mom." Ann Lee hesitated at the door to her bedroom. "Look, I appreciate your concern, but I'm sure if you got to know Michael you would like him. You're just going to have to trust my judgment on this one."

"I *do* trust your judgment. I trust you implicitly. It's that boy I don't trust—and that motorcycle."

"I'll, uh, work on the motorcycle." Ann Lee hastily went into her room and firmly closed the door behind her.

The next day Ann Lee and Susan ran into each other in the locker alcove. "Two people have already asked me if you and Michael are going together," Susan reported. "And Bitsy Ferguson asked me if it was true you're the reason he dumped C.G."

Ann Lee smiled. It was pleasant to be the subject of gossip. She supposed it would be tiresome if it kept up, but right now it gave her the delightful feeling that things were at last starting to happen in her life. She tried hard to stop smiling—she thought of snowstorms, of final exams—but nothing worked. She would have preferred to look faintly bored, but that seemed to be beyond her. "Oh, guess what," she said, picking up her books. "I almost forgot. Bitsy says Math Club is putting my name up for homecoming queen."

"Have they turned the names in yet?"

"Today, I think."

"Maybe I'm not going to be nominated," Susan said anxiously.

"You will be."

"I don't know."

"You will be." Ann Lee smiled.

As Ann Lee left the locker alcove, she reflected that it was very nice to be the one giving the moral support, for a change.

Susan groped blindly in her locker. Nothing was certain in this life, she thought. Jesse was a great pitcher. Everybody knew that, but even he could miss. He had been known to chuck the ball at the water bucket. Similarly, Susan flattered herself that she had a mastery of social life that few could equal. She was careful to psych herself up every morning before getting out of her car so that she could hit the ground smiling. Nobody at West Mount could say she was stuck-up or unfriendly. Even though she did look good and even though she did wear nice clothes, her friendliness disarmed envy. She was bound to be nominated for homecoming queen, wasn't she? She only wished she could be sure.

Suddenly Susan felt an iron grip on her shoulders. She was spun around and thrown against the lockers with a crash. She was horrified to see C.G.'s face jammed up against her own. A sideways glance showed her that C.G.'s fist was drawn back ominously. Susan would have screamed, but she had sucked in her breath so fast from the shock that she couldn't so much as whimper.

The look in C.G.'s eyes changed suddenly. "Oh," she

said. "I thought you were Ann Lee." She dropped Susan and left abruptly.

Trembling, Susan exhaled softly. "Jeez, I'm sure glad I'm *not* Ann Lee."

Suddenly she stiffened. Ann Lee! She had to warn her! She scrabbled hastily through the books in her locker, threw out her English book, scooped it up in a single motion, and ran as fast as she could to homeroom.

"Where's Ann Lee?" she asked Ann Finkernagel as soon as she got to Mrs. Ansley's class.

"Why are you all out of breath?" asked Ann. "Is something wrong?"

"You don't want to know." Susan shivered. "Ann Lee hasn't come in yet?"

"Oh, she came in, but she just dropped a copy of her class pass on Mrs. Ansley's desk and left again. Something about the programs for homecoming. I think they're having a meeting."

"This could be serious," muttered Susan. If Ann Lee wasn't in homeroom, Susan wouldn't see her until lunch. How would she get word to her?

After homeroom she stopped Jenny Montegari in the hall. "If you see Ann Lee, tell her C.G. is looking for her."

Jenny gasped. "No! Oh, my gosh, that's awful. But I'm not going to see her until study hall. Gee, I hope she'll be all right."

A bit later Susan spotted Blake. She fought her way through the mob in the hall, trying to get to him. "Blake!" she yelled.

He turned around and waited for her.

"If you see Ann Lee," she panted when she reached him, "tell her that C.G. is looking for her."

"Why would C.G. be looking for Ann Lee?"

"Use your brain!" cried Susan. "She wants to smash her face. Why else? She grabbed me at my locker this morning thinking I was Ann lee. I thought I was dead meat for sure."

"Well, don't fall apart, Susan. C.G. can't go around beating people up any time she feels like it."

"She can't? Ha! What about Missy Melinik?"

"Besides, Ann Lee's bigger than C.G."

Susan looked at him in eloquent silence while the traffic of the hall flowed around them.

"Okay, I see your point." Blake shrugged uncomfortably. "I guess Ann Lee isn't much of a street fighter, is she? All right, I'll tell her if I see her, but I probably won't see her until lunch."

When Susan went into the cafeteria at lunchtime, she could tell that her message had been delivered because Ann Lee was sitting as stiff as a mannequin, and her flesh was a color somewhere between ivory and avocado.

Susan put her tray down gently on the table. She was a bundle of nerves herself, and she certainly didn't want to make Ann Lee jump.

"It's very simple, Ann Lee," Rainey was explaining patiently. "You can't actually beat her in an open fight, we know that. But what you can do is buy a little time to run."

Susan looked at Ann Lee compassionately. "You got my message, huh?"

"What am I going to do?" wailed Ann Lee. "She's going to kill me."

"I don't think she'll actually kill you," Rainey said.

"Thanks a lot, Rainey. I don't exactly want my face smashed in, either, if you don't mind."

"Look, I keep trying to tell you. You don't have to just stand there while she pounds on you. You can *do* something about it."

Ann Lee smiled wanly. "Life is a pretzel and we only have to bend it, huh? Well, I'll tell you one thing." She slammed her hand resolutely on the table. "I'm not going to give up Michael just because C.G. wants me to."

"Maybe you could get Michael to sort of be your body-guard," said Susan. "She'd never go after you with him there."

"I couldn't do that! Michael and I only have one class together. Besides, I don't want him to know about this."

"Listen to me for a minute, Ann Lee," said Rainey. "I know what I'm talking about. Remember, I used to ride the school bus. You have to keep in mind how simple things, found everywhere, can be weapons." She grabbed the long chain around Susan's neck and wrapped it around her fist, the heavy gold pendant balled in her hand. "Look! Instant brass knuckles."

Susan gagged. "Would you let go of that, Rainey? I need to breathe, if you don't mind."

"Sorry." Rainey released her.

"I don't wear as much jewelry as Susan does," Ann Lee protested.

"You can wear my chain," Susan said. "It was pretty expensive, but let's face it, it's cheaper than plastic surgery."

"A roll of nickels works the same way," Rainey said. "Just improvise."

Ann Lee sighed. "I'm not the brass knuckle type. I've never hit anybody in my life. I'm not even sure I know how to make a fist."

Rainey looked her up and down. "Your shoes! Give me your shoe."

Ann Lee reluctantly stepped out of one shoe.

"The heel is pretty sharp." Rainey tested it against her palm. "You see her coming for you and you take off your shoe. *Voilà!* You're ready to fight. Already you've got a slight tactical edge because she always wears sneakers."

Ann Lee shuddered. "How would I ever get away from her hobbling along on one shoe? I don't even want to think about it."

"I see what you mean. Maybe the shoe is not such a great idea. I know what! A hockey stick."

"I don't play hockey," Ann Lee said wearily.

"But the equipment room is full of hockey sticks. All you have to do is borrow one."

"I don't know, Rainey."

"You've got to be realistic, Ann Lee." Susan leaned toward her and spoke quietly. "I don't want to, like, frighten you or anything, but C.G. thought I was you this morning and she threw me up against the lockers and my whole life flashed before my eyes. I was within an inch of getting totally mangled."

Ann Lee looked down at her fish sticks and coleslaw. She had not eaten a bite.

"I'll get you one of those hockey sticks," Rainey assured her.

"Thank you," Ann Lee said in a small voice.

Blake and Michael came up to the table laughing. "So I said, 'Try me.'"

"Unbelievable."

Balancing his tray on one hand, Michael pulled out a chair. He looked from one girl to the other. "Where's the funeral?"

Ann Lee pushed her fish sticks around with a fork. "Uh, we were just talking about homecoming."

"Oh, yeah. I heard Phalanx Club put up your name, Susan. You two worried about competing against each other or something?"

"Oh, no." Susan gave her brilliant smile automatically. "Whoever wins, it's fine. I'm honored to be nominated."

"I just thought you all looked a little down." Michael looked from one girl to the other again.

"No, everything's fine." Susan shot a warning look at Blake.

"Sure." Ann Lee squirted ketchup on her fish sticks and immediately regretted it. It struck her that ketchup looked a lot like blood.

"Is there some reason you're just wearing one shoe?" Michael asked her.

She looked down at her bare foot. "I was hot?" She hastily slipped the shoe back on her foot.

Jesse slid his tray onto the table and sat down. "Coach Delaney kept me after class. He wants me to look into baseball scholarships for college." He looked at Susan expectantly. "Well, what do you think?"

"Sounds like a good idea."

"I thought you'd like the idea."

"I do."

"You don't sound as if you like it."

"Well, I do."

"It would give me some time to develop some consistency, and that college degree would be something to fall back on if baseball doesn't work out for me because of injuries or whatever."

"I see. Yes, it really seems like a good idea. Yes."

Michael shot a meaningful look at Jesse. "I think this homecoming junk just possibly is sending some people who shall be nameless right around the bend. What do you think?"

"I guess we have got a lot on our minds." Ann Lee gave him a wobbly smile.

TEN

_T_hat afternoon Ann Lee borrowed a pair of sunglasses from Tony Sandow and two rubber bands from Mrs. Finney in the office. With her hair in braids and her face half hidden by Tony's shades, she thought she looked quite different. It was entirely possible that C.G. would not even recognize her. However, she decided to take the most roundabout route imaginable to the parking lot as an added precaution. It would obviously be better if she could avoid running into C.G.

She tucked her books under one arm, the hockey stick under the other, and sneaked from A wing to the band room. After a quick reconnaissance, she proceeded cautiously from the band room to the cafeteria building and stood there for a moment, breathing heavily.

She was by then within sight of the parking lot. Standing

in the shadow of the cafeteria building, she saw kids in the parking lot throwing books into their cars and driving off— carefree, happy kids. How she envied them!

So far it had been fairly easy, but now she had to gather her nerve for the final dash across open ground to her car. She sucked in her breath and ran as fast as she could, stumbling a bit in her haste. When she got to her car she had her keys ready in a second and then she had her door unlocked. But before she could crawl in, a hand grasped her shoulder. Her flesh turned to goose bumps and her knees buckled.

"Hey," C.G. growled in her ear.

Ann Lee spun around suddenly. "Violence is not the answer!" she cried.

C.G. laughed. "Oh, yeah?" She drew back her fist.

Without thinking, Ann Lee lifted the hockey stick and banged C.G. hard on the shoulder. She didn't wait to see the effect—she was too busy getting into her car. She jumped in, snapped down the lock button, and jammed the key in the ignition. C.G. banged angrily on the car door and tried the handle. Ann Lee tried hard not to think of what it would be like if C.G. broke the car window.

The car's engine leapt to life and smoke blew out the exhaust. Ann Lee breathed a prayer of thanks that she had not flooded the engine.

"Hey!" yelled C.G.

But Ann Lee was backing her car out of the parking place. She was safe! C.G. could not get her now. Glancing behind her to make sure C.G. wasn't chasing her, she drove out of the parking lot. She bent over the wheel as she joined the slow-moving line of cars leaving school. Soon she would be within sight of the teachers posted along the road as traffic wardens. Even C.G. must see it was pointless to pursue her. "Stupid, stupid," she muttered to herself. "I should have known she'd wait by the car. All that sneaking around was wasted. Naturally, she'd just wait for me there." It had felt so strange to let her books slide to the pavement and drive off without them. But this was no time to worry about books.

When she finally got off the school grounds, she drove directly home. Her heart was thumping as if it were trying to leap out of her chest. She went inside, taking care to lock the front door of the house behind her. Then she went to the upstairs bathroom and took two aspirin. She lay down on her bed, shoes and all, feeling weak and faint. Suddenly the phone beside her bed rang and she jumped. After a moment she propped herself up on an elbow and answered it. She held the receiver a couple of inches from her ear because she half expected to hear C.G.'s voice uttering a bloodcurdling threat.

"Ann Lee? This is Susan. I just wanted to see if you got home all right."

Ann Lee licked her lips. "Barely. She almost got me in the parking lot, but I was able to hold her off a second with one blow of the hockey stick. What do you think, Susan? Can I take a hockey stick with me to all my classes from now on? I mean, for the rest of the year? For the rest of my life, even?"

"I don't see why not. Phil Morton carries that teddy bear."

"I dropped my books during my getaway. I hope they didn't get all banged up. Do you think you could go by the parking lot and get them for me?"

"I'll ask Jesse to get them. Don't worry about it."

"You realize what this means, don't you? I'm going to have to live like one of those people who are targeted by terrorists. I'll have to take a different route to school every day, hire bodyguards, check my car for bombs, take karate lessons. I never dreamed having a boyfriend was going to be like this."

"Come on now. C.G. can't stay mad at you forever. Besides, by now she's probably trashed your books and she's feeling a lot better."

Ann Lee whimpered. C.G.'s angry face swam before her eyes. It was all too easy to imagine her stomping on the books, mutilating them. That was the kind of person she was. "I don't know if I can handle this, Susan."

"Hey, give yourself a little credit. You fought off C.G. Bowman! Not everybody can say that."

"She was really surprised when I bopped her with the hockey stick," Ann Lee admitted. "She didn't know I'd be armed."

"See? You can handle her. You'll be fine, you'll see. But we've got to have Bitsy Ferguson spread the word that you were *not* the reason Michael dumped her."

"Do you really think that would help?"

"Well, it can't hurt."

"Excuse me, I have to lie down for a minute. I think I'm starting to hyperventilate."

"Jesse and I will give you a ride back and forth from school tomorrow, if that's any help," offered Susan. "We'll even walk with you to homeroom, okay?"

"That would be good. Thanks."

After Ann Lee hung up, she lay trembling a moment.

"Ann Lee!" Mrs. Smith called. "You home?"

"I'm home," called Ann Lee. "Up here, Mom."

Her mother opened the door of the bedroom. "Are you sick, sweetheart? What are you doing in bed?"

"Something's going around." Ann Lee wrinkled her nose and tried an experimental sniffle. "I may have to stay home from school for a long, long time."

"Maybe I'd better take your temperature."

"You only have a temperature if your body is fighting back. I think mine has given up."

Her mother looked worried. "Maybe we'd better take you to the doctor and have him look at you."

Ann Lee turned her face to the wall. "Maybe I can limp along for a few more days." She sighed. "I really don't like to get behind in my schoolwork."

The truth was, she wasn't sure what would be the best thing to do. It would be nice to stay out of school for a few days; the idea was attractive. But wasn't it possible that a few days of doing nothing but lying around in bed might dull her reflexes? That might make it harder for her to get away in a pinch!

"My poor baby," cooed her mother. "I'll just pull the blinds so you can rest for a little while."

Ann Lee lay on her bed in the semidarkness for a few minutes after her mother left, but her mind was filled with horrible imaginings—C.G. with a knife between her teeth, C.G. accompanied by a pit bull. Finally, unable to stand her own thoughts a minute longer, she switched on the light and fished a beat-up paperback from under her bed. She would not have confessed it to just anyone, but she sometimes immersed herself in the adventures of Monique when things got rough. Monique was a fiery redhead who, dressed only in a bustier and strategically arranged tatters, adorned the cover of her favorite book, *Monique and the Black Baron*. Monique spoke five languages—English, Russian, Portuguese, and Eldomo, an obscure dialect spoken in the mining towns of South Africa. She had doelike green eyes, sensuous lips, and a voluptuous figure. Naturally, every man who met her fell in love with her. Ann Lee used to think that Monique's effect on men was what was most enviable about her. But now, upon mature reflection, she decided that even better than having Monique's sex appeal would be having her skill in unarmed combat. She opened the novel and began to read: "Struggling, Monique freed her arm and pressed on the pulsing blue artery in Lord Ebony's neck. He at once slumped and fell helpless to the ground. His knife clattered, useless, onto the paving stones." Yeah! Attagirl! Ann Lee snuggled down into the covers and turned the page.

The next day Ann Lee had to go to the office before school and pay for her books. Jesse had found no trace of them in the parking lot.

"How could you lose three books at one time, Ann Lee?" asked Mrs. Finney. She pushed the necessary forms across the counter.

"I had a bad day."

"What sort of bad day could make you lose three books?" Mrs. Finney peered over the counter. "Is that a hockey stick? I didn't realize you were interested in sports."

"Sort of." Ann Lee quickly signed the forms and hurried out of the office before Mrs. Finney could ask any more awkward questions. But as she went to homeroom, she had the sensation that people were looking at her. She wondered if the story was all over school that C.G. was gunning for her. Was that pity she detected in people's eyes?

"Hi, there!" Bitsy Ferguson pounced on her. "Is it true that C.G. attacked you in the parking lot and then made a bonfire of all your books?"

Ann Lee sighed. The tale of her difficulty was all over school all right. "Well, I don't know what happened to the books, to be honest. C.G. did go after me, but I was able to fight her off and get away."

Bitsy looked Ann Lee up and down to check for damage. "It doesn't look as if she broke any bones. I wonder what she'll do next. Aren't you just *petrified?*"

Ann Lee hoisted the hockey stick to her shoulder and tried her best to imagine how Monique would feel in such a situation. "I'm not afraid of C.G.," she said stoutly.

"Wow," said Bitsy.

For a moment Ann Lee almost believed her own words. She had the hockey stick, didn't she? She even swaggered slightly as she walked to homeroom. She sat down next to Susan.

"So far so good!" Susan whispered. "I think burning your books really got it all out of C.G.'s system. You probably don't have anything to worry about now."

Mrs. Ansley called roll. "Orders for homecoming corsages should be turned in as soon as possible," she announced. "Corsages will be delivered sixth period on Friday."

"You really think maybe C.G.'s done all she's going to do?" whispered Ann Lee.

"Makes sense to me."

Ann Lee took what comfort she could in Susan's opinion.

But after homeroom she had a bad moment when she spotted C.G. coming out of a locker alcove. Ann Lee flattened herself against the wall to protect her flanks. Quaking, she hoisted the hockey stick to her shoulder. The boy at the water fountain squirted himself full in the face, and a couple of girls near her stepped back hastily.

Ann Lee began to feel like the victim in a stalker movie. Her grip on the hockey stick tightened.

C.G. looked at Ann Lee steadily, her black eyes seeming to burn from within. Then she smiled a little and walked on.

Ann Lee shivered. She wanted to grab at people as they passed by and ask them what they thought it meant. That smile! It was not a friendly smile, was it? Yet C.G. had not actually made a hostile move. She had walked past. Was that only because she saw the hockey stick?

Ann Lee cleared her throat. "Well, I guess that's it," she said loudly. Several people stared at her, but nobody said a word. She shrugged and tried to look unconcerned. Her knees felt wobbly all the way to her class.

At lunch she told Rainey what had happened.

"So what do you think?" she asked. "Do you think Susan's right when she says that burning my books got the anger out of C.G.'s system? Tell me what you think! Tell me the truth. Whatever it is, I can take it."

"I don't know. I guess what I think is maybe you stood up to her, showed her you wouldn't be pushed around, and so she's backing down."

Ann Lee envied Rainey's coolness. Of course, it was easy for Rainey to be calm, since she wasn't on C.G.'s hit list. But Ann Lee never remembered seeing Rainey look frightened. She always had her chin tilted a little as if she was ready to take on anyone.

Ann Lee cleared her throat. "I think I'll carry the hockey stick around with me for a little while longer, just in case."

Tucker suddenly pulled out a chair and sat down. "What's going on, Rainey? Can't we even talk? Why aren't you ever at home when I call?"

Rainey avoided his eyes. "I'm pretty busy."

Ann Lee heartily wished she were somewhere else. It was awkward being the third wheel. She felt like an eavesdropper.

"We're still friends, aren't we?" he asked.

"Sure."

"Well, why don't we go to homecoming together? We can have dinner at Gino's before the game."

"I'm sorry, Tucker." Rainey smiled at him. "I've already made plans."

"You're going with Blake, aren't you? He's been telling you stuff about me."

Michael plumped himself down heavily and the table shook. "Hi ya, Tucker, old bean. Why don't you go play in traffic or something?"

Tucker flushed. "Nice to see you, too, Dessaseaux." He stood up.

After he had gone, Michael put his arm around Ann Lee. "Okay, okay, I know what you're thinking. You're thinking I was unkind, rude, thoughtless. Just keep in mind that I am only thinking of the greater good. Do we really want Blake to come up and find Tucker at the table? I mean, let's face it. Something about Tucker just rattles his cage. What can I say?"

"I hope we can all act civilized," Rainey said stiffly.

Michael raised his eyebrows. "One girl, two guys—that's not a prescription for civilization. That's a prescription for the Trojan War."

Blake brought his tray to the table. His eyes were merry, so apparently he had not seen Tucker. "Say-hey, Ann Lee, I heard—"

"You're right, Blake," Ann Lee chimed in hastily. "We *have* sold almost enough advertisements to meet our goal. I wonder if your father would care to take a small ad."

"What would the ad say? Two-for-one special on gall bladders?" Blake grinned.

"Usually they say 'Compliments of so and so,' " Ann Lee said firmly. "Simple, tasteful, and it does help pay for the printing of each player's picture at the back of the program, which is what we all want, isn't it?"

"I'll ask my dad about it." Blake looked at her curiously, but to her relief he didn't try again to introduce the subject of C.G.'s attack on her.

She felt a faint tickling sensation as Michael lifted a strand of her hair and let it fall.

"So tell me, O light of my heart, what do you fancy for a corsage? Chrysanthemums? Roses? Ragweed?"

Ann Lee felt her face grow warm. "Anything would be lovely. Except maybe ragweed."

"Picky, picky." He smiled at her.

Ann Lee felt happiness wash over her. It was all worth it, she decided. The motorcycle, C.G.—she could handle it. She was sure she could.

ELEVEN

*F*riday was homecoming. Corsages were delivered to the sixth period classes, each with an oblong tag attached saying who had ordered it and who was to receive it. Mrs. Philpot passed them out in English class. "Mary Ann, Keesha, Yolanda, Rainey." She went down the rows laying the corsages on the girls' desks. "Have I forgotten anybody? Wait a minute, Rainey, you have two."

On Rainey's desk, a corsage of crimson roses clashed strongly with an oversize yellow mum.

"Those are both for you?" asked Mrs. Philpot.

Rainey nodded mutely.

"Oh. Well, all right. I think that's everyone. Now, please notice the assignment on the board, people. The world doesn't come to a stop just because this is homecoming weekend, you know."

Bitsy Ferguson jumped to her feet. "Don't forget the parade and the pep rally right after school, you guys. And the bonfire is at six-thirty. As vice-president of the Phalanx Club I want to urge everybody to attend."

The bell rang and the students shuffled to their feet.

"Who are they from?" Sondra Mason stopped at Rainey's desk. "Do you have a secret admirer or something?"

Rainey shrugged noncommittally.

Watching this from the back of the room, Blake simmered. As he gathered up his books, the room suddenly seemed unbearably hot. He knew who had sent those roses. They had to be from Tucker, that jerk. Didn't the creep get the message? Rainey had dumped him. It was all over between them. And now red roses. What was that supposed to mean? He had a nerve. All that junk she had going with Tucker was just temporary insanity. Red roses, for crying out loud. Blake thought of how he'd like to see Tucker on a slow boat to China.

"Jeez, watch where you're going, Farraby."

"Sorry." Blake bent to pick up Kevin Reese's papers, his mind churning with incoherent thoughts. Roses! What a show-off Tucker was! He hated to think what roses cost. But one thing was for sure—he would not ask Rainey about them. If she wanted to tell him something, she could tell him. He wasn't going to ask.

Blake was the last one out of the room. When he passed Mrs. Philpot's desk, he saw the corsage of roses lying among the crumpled papers in the wastebasket. He didn't know whether that made him feel better or worse. You had to feel pretty strongly about somebody to throw away good flowers, didn't you?

When he got out to the parking lot he squinted against the bright sunlight, looking for Rainey. He shifted his books awkwardly to his other arm, feeling the heat on his head and through the soles of his shoes. It was warm, all right, but it was warmth without any promise, an Indian summer. The night would be chilly. Blake felt as if the outer layer of his skin had been peeled away, exposing his nerves. He was irritable and, most of all, unhappy.

At last he spotted Rainey's car. She was unlocking her door, having taken a practically unnecessary precaution, in Blake's eyes, given the age and condition of the car. He jogged over to her and let out his breath. "Are you on your way to work?"

"I don't have to go to work. I'm working Saturday, so I have today off."

"Well, why don't we go get something to eat, then?"

She glanced uncertainly behind her.

"We can come back for your car later," he said. "So don't worry about that."

"Okay. Hang on." She tossed her books in the backseat. "I'd better take the corsage with me. I don't want to leave it in the car where it might wilt in the heat."

She turned to smile at him and for an instant her blue-black hair caught fire in the sunshine. Blake felt his stomach twist in a pang of regret. He wished fiercely that he had been the one to send her the roses. He would like to have given her armfuls of red roses to braid into her hair.

The roar of a crowd sounded ominously behind him, as if a riot had erupted in the gym. "Pep rally's taking off, I guess," he commented.

"Do you want to go to it?" she asked.

"Nah. I've been to my share of pep rallies. Now that I'm a senior, I'm retiring."

They walked over to his car. Blake felt clumsy and stupid. Worse, his mind was so full of roses he wasn't sure he could think of anything to say. He kept stealing glances at her out of the corner of his eye as he put the top of the car down. Rainey carefully laid the plastic corsage case behind the bucket seats. Blake waited for her to say something about Tucker's roses. He watched the soft movement of the fabric of her blouse and noticed that her lips were slightly parted, but she didn't say anything. He was consumed by wild regret. The surge of emotion frightened him. He had done everything wrong with Rainey, everything. The loan. The summer. The corsage. The only thing he had going for him was that she was still his friend. He gritted his teeth. That would have to be enough. He would just have to go on from there.

He looked away from her, toward the gym. "At least with everybody at the pep rally it should be easy to get out of the parking lot, for a change."

"I know. It looks as if almost everybody is staying for it."

Blake slid in behind the wheel. He was relieved to discover that this simple action made him feel more in control of himself. Sometimes it was as if the Corvette represented his better self—the part that didn't screw up. "So," he said, "I guess about now Michael and his crew are lining up floats in the gym while everybody screams, 'Kill East Gate! Smash 'em, mangle 'em.' Has it hit you that school spirit is sort of primitive?"

"Well, sure." Rainey smiled. "But I don't think you'd get people very churned up with a cheer that said, 'Negotiate. Work it out. Compromise!'"

"You may have something there." Blake turned the key in the ignition. He didn't want to go on making stupid small talk about traffic and pep rallies. He wanted her to tell him what those red roses meant to her. The big engine purred as he steered out of the parking lot. The school's entrance road was startlingly empty, with no sign of teachers with walkie-talkies. A few hardwood trees showed in the pine woods beside the road, their leaves turning yellow and orange. They passed the sign saying West Mount High School. "I wish they'd have a pep rally every day. Not a bit of traffic," Blake commented. "This is great."

As soon as he got out on Baker Street, he picked up speed. The wind made Rainey's dark hair fly behind her and whipped it into her face. He would have loved to know what she was thinking, but he tried to keep from looking at her and concentrated grimly on the road. She would tell him if she wanted to. Despite his determination not to ask, to his horror, he heard himself saying hoarsely, "Did Tucker send you the roses?"

"Yup. I can't imagine what was going on in his pea-brained little mind to send them to me. I just pitched them in the trash. Do you think I should have sent them to a nursing home or something like that?"

When Blake shot Rainey a quick sideways glance, he saw that her brow was creased in puzzlement. "I did sort of hate to waste them," she went on, "but I was afraid he would see me with them and think there was some sort of symbolism in me hanging on to them or something."

Blake took a deep breath. "Nah, you did the right thing to pitch them. You couldn't have done better—except maybe you could have ground them under the heel of your shoe."

Rainey's eyes danced, and Blake felt the tension flow out of his body as he stepped on the gas. The reflections of the yellow and the white lines on the road met in a V on the car's gleaming red hood as the road disappeared quickly under them. Rainey really did seem perfectly matter-of-fact about throwing the roses away. It had to be a good sign. The Corvette sped down Baker Street and his sense of well-being grew.

A minute later he slowed down. "I keep forgetting they're still working on Baker Street just past the shopping center. They're widening it. I'm going to try to cut around the construction area or we'll be stuck here five minutes."

A horn blared at them as the Corvette ran the yellow light and turned off Baker Street.

The sound of the traffic faded behind them. Blake drove along the leafy tree–lined street north of the thoroughfare. They went past wide lawns and then past a big sign announcing West Mount Baptist Church.

"I haven't been down this street in forever." Rainey combed her hair away from her face with her fingers and looked around with interest. When she pointed to the right, her hair at once was whipped into her face by the wind, but she didn't seem to mind. "Look, Blake! There's our old school."

He slowed way down. "Hey, I remember that place." He and Rainey had attended Slow Creek for only a couple of years before the schools were redistricted.

"Back then the teachers were always trying to get us to share things with each other, remember? I sure haven't heard anybody talk about sharing lately. Now all I hear about is the SATs. You know, smash your competition, climb to the top. I mean, when I think about it I actually miss the second grade. Do you remember Mrs. West? She used to stick her fingers in her ears and say 'Inside voices, boys and girls! Inside voices!' I guess we were pretty loud.''

"I remember she was fat. Billy Tomkins always used to steal my snack,'' said Blake. "And I kept wishing he'd steal Mrs. West's snack instead because she sure didn't need hers. No wonder it took me so long to get my growth spurt. I was probably running a major calorie deficit.'' He slowed down even more and they crept past the sprawling one-story brick building. A slide and a volleyball court were at one end of the playground. The other end of the playground was dominated by a substantial set of swings. The ground under each swing was deeply cupped, scooped out by countless dragging feet.

"Remember those swings?'' Rainey exclaimed. "I always used to want to swing during the whole recess. That's all I ever wanted to do. I'd run to get to them first and because I was little and fast, I usually made it. But half the time some dumb teacher would come out and say, 'Now, let's share the swings, boys and girls.' Of course, I didn't want to share. I'd just about killed myself getting to the swing in the first place. And I never noticed any of the teachers sharing. I mean, heck, they didn't even drive in car pools!''

Blake pulled his car up on the grass and switched the engine off. "Well, now you don't have to share. Want to swing?''

She looked at him. "You aren't kidding? You really want to swing?''

"Sure.''

"Okay.'' She grinned. They got out and walked through the rough grass. Small winged insects flew up, disturbed by their steps. "Doesn't everything look a lot smaller than it used to?'' She looked around. "I used to think if you swung high enough you'd go all the way around. I used to swing really high, and I had this feeling I was living dangerously. You know, life in the fast lane, second grade style. I guess I thought I was going to go into orbit or something.''

"Like how we used to think if you dug a hole deep enough you'd get to China. I was sure of it back then. It just seemed logical.'' He shook his head mournfully.

"I tried that! I worked on it for days—weeks, maybe. Anyway, a long time. It was a big project, me and the kitchen spoon. I was really determined, but it didn't work. I never did get to China.''

"I remember we used to think if you stepped on a Lucky Strike package you'd have good luck. Those Lucky Strike packages were hard to find, probably because of the surgeon general's report. And I used to think chicken pox would be cured by chickens. I mean, why else would it be called chicken pox? Boy, I had it all figured out.''

The seats of the swings were made of heavy wood and were attached to thick, long chains suspended from a metal framework. Rainey and Blake pushed off with their feet, beginning slowly, then pumped until they were going quite high.

After a few minutes Blake let go of his swing when it was at the highest point of its arc, sailed through the air, and made a four-point landing on the grass. "Oooph!'' The shock of the landing ran through his joints with a jolt. He hoped he hadn't torn a tendon.

Rainey landed near him, breathless and laughing, and rolled over. "Ouch!'' She winced. "This ground is a lot harder than I remember.''

"Yeah, to think I used to jump out of those swings all the time.'' Blake leaned on an elbow and watched her.

Rainey plucked a blade of grass and began shredding it into

narrow strips. "Golly, it's been a long time since I've been on a swing. That was fun." She let the tattered grass fall and plucked up another blade. "If we had daisies we could make a daisy chain. Keesha Davis and I used to get in a lot of trouble in gym when the class played softball because we'd get out in the outfield and talk and make daisy chains. One time Coach Hollins screamed at us: 'If I look out there and see one more person picking daisies, I'm going to have to take steps.' I never did figure out what he meant. Maybe he was going to go after those daisies with a lawn mower."

Blake shifted his position. "I know what. Why don't I read your palm?"

"You read palms?"

"You don't have to look at me like I'm nuts. Why shouldn't I be able to read palms? Give me one good reason."

"I thought it was just Gypsy ladies who did that."

"That's prejudice, pure and simple, Rainey. I've noticed there's an idea going around that white guys can't do much of anything. They're not supposed to be able to jump or sprint or stuff a basket or play jazz or take care of babies or have intuition or read fortunes or anything. I'm here to tell you it's all prejudice. Give me your hand—money-back guarantee."

Warily, she held her hand out to him. With his forefinger he traced the line that marked the crease of her thumb. "This is your life line. You see how it's long and it intersects with lot of other lines?"

"That's good?"

"Very good. You'll have an interesting life. Now you see this less definite line that sort of echoes it, but meets the cross line? That's your love line." He ran his finger gently along it and frowned. "Only thing is, I can't quite tell if it says Tucker or Blake."

"I don't think much of your fortune-telling, then. Tucker should be in the, uh"—she glanced at the palm of her hand—"the *history* line. Is that what all this palm reading is about? You want to talk about Tucker?"

"Nope, not really. It's just an excuse to hold your hand."

Rainey lifted his hand to her cheek and gently brushed it against her face. "You don't need an excuse to do that."

Suddenly Blake's breath was ragged, as if he'd been running. The gesture spoke of such trust and closeness that it knocked him out.

"Why are you worrying about Tucker?" She looked at him curiously.

"I don't know. It's me. I guess I'm a mass of insecurities. It's crazy. Forget it. I don't want to talk about it anymore."

"Inside, we're all crazy, you know? Let me tell you something funny." She stretched out, then propped herself up on an elbow. "When you said you were going to read my palm, I believed you. I mean, I had this really funny feeling that—I mean, sometimes I think—" She hesitated, then rushed on, "Are you a psychic, Blake?"

He recoiled. "No! Good grief, what gave you an idea like that? Okay, I won't tell anybody I can read palms anymore, I promise. Jeez!"

She frowned. "It's just that sometimes you seem to hear what I don't say. You know what I mean? I've had this sensation that you're reading my mind. I guess that sounds crazy. Actually, now that I think it over, it *is* crazy. Forget I said anything."

"Nah, that's not crazy. For that there's a simple explanation."

"You do it with mirrors?"

"Nope, I'm interested."

"What?"

"I'm interested. I watch you a lot."

"I've got a poker face!"

He shook his head. "No, you haven't."

Rainey's face grew pink. "Well, anyway, if you can read my mind, you know that Tucker is ancient history."

"Good. That's what I want to hear." He realized that his self-confidence, never as strong as it should have been, had taken a severe beating when Rainey defected to Tucker over the summer. He wondered if he would ever be able to put Tucker out of his mind.

Rainey scrambled to her feet and dusted bits of dry grass off her jeans. "We better get moving. Remember, the homecoming game is tonight."

Blake made a face and pushed himself up. "As if anybody could forget." He ached in several places. It was very possible, he decided, that he was getting entirely too big to jump out of a swing like a second-grader.

TWELVE

Two, four, six, eight, who do we appreciate?'' screamed the cheerleaders. Rainey and Blake heard them clearly all the way back at the concession stand. It was halftime at the homecoming game, and West Mount had finished the first half three points behind.

Not that Rainey cared about the score. She sneaked a glance at Blake. Everything seemed different to her after this afternoon, and she wondered if he felt it, too.

She had been stunned to see the fear and desolation in his eyes when he asked her about the roses Tucker had sent. Who would have guessed he would be so jealous? Jealous to the point of being sick.

It would have been funny if it hadn't hurt him so much. She had always seen Blake as invulnerable. His looks, his car, the money he had lent her, his smashing serve in tennis—to her it meant he must feel a bit superior. She had imagined that inside he felt set for life. That must have bothered her more than she knew because when she saw him falling apart, she was rocked. Suddenly the air between them became charged and every move, every word, was heavy with meaning. In an outpouring of warmth that astonished her, she longed to touch him. It was as if, for the first time, in the package of her good feelings for Blake all lights were blazing and the batteries had been included.

Right at this moment she wanted to put her arms around him. She was prevented only by her deep and abiding fear of looking foolish.

She looked down at the huge yellow mum on her houndstooth check jacket and swallowed. She wished he would say something. "It looks like we're the only people in the stadium who want hot dogs," she offered. The sharp smell of mustard pierced the air and underneath it was the toasty smell of peanuts. She looked around the deserted concession stand, feeling its loneliness. Beyond the stands the stadium lights cast a bright haze into the night sky.

"Naturally." Blake handed her a hot dog. "They all want to see the homecoming queen crowned."

Her eyes searched his face. "Don't we want to see that, too?"

"There's no rush. You know how long this kind of thing takes. First they'll drive the girls around the field in convertibles, and then the band will play some more and the announcer will do a big build-up; then there'll be the alma mater and junk. We'll have lots of time to eat." Blake bit into his hot dog as they walked together back toward the bleachers.

The stands were teeming and not just with students. The mothers of football players, their legs wrapped in blankets, sat stoically with pink noses. Nearby sat worried-looking fathers. A couple of the more determined fathers were positioned on the ground with camcorders and auxiliary lights. Grade-school kids ran back and forth in front of the stands, tripping on light cords. Guys grunted wisely to one another about offense and defense while girls in wool skirts and blazers deployed their programs defensively to protect their clothes from dripping mustard. The community had turned out en masse for the annual ritual of homecoming. Even a sprinkling of college freshmen had shown up, having sprouted fraternity pins and sophistication.

The cheerleaders, their green and blue gored skirts a blur, whirled into a frenzy of cartwheels. "Let's hear it for West Mount!" they shrieked.

The stands erupted in an explosion of screaming and stomping. Standing beside the bleachers, Rainey felt the vibrations travel through her body until her head ached with the noise. She darted a glance at Blake, wishing she could read his face. Everything had seemed so clear and simple to her that afternoon, but now she was in need of reassurance.

"Go, West Mount," screamed the fans, until finally the cheerleaders flopped down on their bench, exhausted.

Out on the field, trumpets blared, "Time is on my side." West Mount's band director had seen no incongruity in having the funky little melody played by a full brass band. "Ti-ime is on my side," the clarinets echoed, dragging the notes.

In an abrupt motion Blake pitched his hot dog into a trash barrel. "Let's dance," he said.

"Here?" Rainey was startled. "Right here by the bleachers?"

"Why not? Nobody's looking at us. Come on." He put his arms around her. The thin paper wrapping from a straw drifted down from the seats over them like a bit of giant confetti. Flattened paper cups crunched under Rainey's feet. In the shadow of the bleachers they were shielded from the harsh stadium lights. When Rainey leaned her head against Blake's chest, she could feel his heart beating. She held her breath and listened to it.

"Rainey?"

She looked up.

"You're my favorite girl, you know that?" His voice was husky. "You won't go away again, will you?"

She shook her head, her eyes fastened wonderingly on his face.

"Because"—his voice broke—"if you do, I just don't think I can take it."

She touched her fingers to his cheek. "I'm not going anywhere." Pressing against him, she felt the warmth inside her spread to her fingers and toes.

"I probably shouldn't ask this," he said in a rush, "but this isn't just some sort of weird revenge scheme against Tucker, is it?"

She pulled away and grinned up at him. She hated to see Blake unhappy, but the whole thing did have its funny side. "You are crazy, Blake. Sure! Right! My going out with you is just a way to make Tucker jealous."

"Don't even say it," he said gruffly. "It's not funny."

"Well, you don't believe it, do you?"

She was relieved to see that he didn't. Not really. She wanted this to be the end of all talk about Tucker. She wanted to forget Tucker had ever existed, because thinking about him made her feel just plain stupid.

Blake squeezed her. "God, I think I'm in love with you," he said. "Does that scare you to death?"

She shook her head. All her misgivings had fallen away gently like the petals of an overblown rose. She only wanted to be close to him.

"Woo-oo," yelled a little boy overhead. "Wooo-oo-oo!"

Blake glanced up, then pulled her underneath the bleachers. From there she could see the aluminum bottoms of the seats. When she looked around she saw swatches of wool skirts sticking through the slats and pale fat legs pressed against the panels.

"The things you have to do to get some privacy these days!" complained Blake.

A giggle welled up in Rainey's throat. She hadn't quite imagined true love coming to her under the bleachers.

His lips brushed gently against her forehead. Then he kissed her lingeringly.

Rainey caught a movement out of the corner of her eye. "What was that?" Alarmed, she looked over her shoulder.

"What was what?"

"Over there. You didn't see it? I saw a shadow out of the corner of my eye—it was sort of slinking past us."

Blake laughed softly. "That wasn't a shadow. That was C. G. Bowman."

"What's she up to?" Rainey shivered.

"Who cares?" He blew a stray hair out of her face and drew her toward him.

She forgot C.G. All her fears, all her unhappiness about Blake's lending her money seemed to belong to long ago. None of it mattered anymore. All that counted now was that Blake needed her. "Ti-ime is on my side," sang the trumpets.

At the edge of the field, the members of the homecoming court and their escorts stood shivering. Each girl wore a chrysanthemum the size of a cabbage. A breeze swept over the field from the north and found them standing beside the locker room. The petals of the chrysanthemums shivered, and the girls clutched desperately at their hair.

"I wish I'd worn long underwear." Michael puffed warm breath onto his fingers.

"Okay," said Mrs. Enwright. "Escorts, come over here. Each of you will pick up a bouquet of roses, then walk on out to the fifty-yard line." Mrs. Enwright was a thin, harassed-looking woman with flyaway gray hair and the disposition of a drill sergeant. "Get going. Move it! Now, Ann Lee and Susan, you get in the white car. Mona and Keesha, you get in the red one. Remember, you boys who are driving—drive slow! We don't want to lose anybody tonight. Drive directly in front of the stands, then let your girls out in the center at the fifty-yard line and come back immediately for the next two."

"Yeah, yeah," said the boy in the white Mercedes. "We know all that already. We've been over it a thousand times."

Mrs. Enwright glared at him.

Susan tottered over to the car. Her high heels took careful managing on the turf. She had to put all her weight on her toes or the heels would sink in and she would end up skewered to the ground. She and Ann Lee clambered into the Mercedes and perched on the top of the backseat. "All set?" asked the boy at the wheel in a bored voice. Without waiting for their answer, he put his foot on the gas, and the car began to move slowly away. Susan hugged herself tight and exchanged an uncertain smile with Ann Lee.

Her nose was icy when the Mercedes drove out onto the open football field. Ann Lee reminded herself that this was a proud moment. That wasn't easy to remember when her teeth were chattering. As the white convertible drove toward the stands, the football field seemed as vast and empty as the Gobi Desert and about equally inviting. The band at the east side of the field looked insignificant and impossibly far away. "Ladies and gentlemen, the homecoming court," boomed the voice over the loudspeaker. "Miss Ann Lee Smith. Miss Susan Brantley."

As the Mercedes passed before the bleachers, Susan saw only indistinguishable patches of color up at the top tiers, but she could make out some actual people on the lower rows. She stretched her mouth in an approximation of a smile, and the cold air hit her teeth. She raised her hand and waved it back and forth slowly. Glancing over her shoulder, she saw Mona and Keesha in the Jaguar behind them.

Susan's hand began to feel numb and bloodless. She lifted her other hand and kept on waving. Her resolute smile held steady. The notes of "A Pretty Girl Is Like a Melody" wafted across the field. It was hard to smile at an indistinguishable crowd, so she tried to pick out particular individuals. "Hi!" she squealed to the cheerleaders. "Hi!" She wiggled her fingers at the fathers with the camcorders.

She saw that under the stadium lights Ann Lee's face looked splotchy with cold and her lipstick had turned magenta. Susan shivered and turned away, hoping she didn't look like that.

At last they had reached the far end of the stands. At once

the car doubled back and deposited them in the center of the field at the fifty yard line. Jesse and Michael waited there with the other boys. They didn't look much like themselves in their good suits, their faces pale in the artificial light. Jesse handed Susan her bouquet of roses, looking profoundly relieved to be rid of it.

Susan cradled the roses in one arm, still smiling, and reminded herself to keep her shoulders back even though the breeze seemed to be finding its way between the buttons of her jacket and she felt an almost overwhelming impulse to hunch over. Jesse said something to her. She couldn't make out the words, but she caught the warm and comforting tone that meant he was on her side. Suddenly she swelled with pride and inclined her head toward the crowd, glorying in her moment in the spotlight. I *am* honored to be here, she thought, surprised. For a moment she felt so good she almost forgot that she was cold. She leaned toward Ann Lee. "Are you nervous?"

"A little." Actually, Ann Lee felt faintly sick to her stomach. She hated being conspicuous. The only thing that comforted her was that the people in the stands were so far away that most of them could barely see her. She gazed up at Michael, thinking how massive he looked and, with his gray hair, distinguished. He caught her eye and winked, and she felt herself melt with pleasure. She was glad she had never told him about the trouble she'd had with C.G. It was bad enough for her to be standing there worrying without him worrying, too. This should have been the proudest moment of her high school career. But instead of feeling proud she felt like—well, a sitting duck! She pushed the thought away.

A voice on the loudspeaker announced the names of the remaining members of the homecoming court. Four more girls stepped out of cars and took bouquets from their escorts.

"Look!" Jesse nudged Susan. "Over there."

Susan made out something rather shapeless and blue over the south end of the stands. She squinted at it but couldn't make out what it was. Something rather big and soft. Maybe it was a tarpaulin billowing in the breeze.

"What is it?" she asked. But as she strained to see it she began to discern that it was shaped like a light bulb, narrow-waisted at the bottom but billowing out to roundness above. As she watched, it grew more round, even taut.

"It looks like a hot air balloon to me," said Jesse. "A smallish one."

The balloon wrinkled a bit and sank, but then it filled out again and began to rise steadily. Once aloft, it slowly drifted out in front of the bleachers. The stadium lights made it glisten faintly. She could see then that Jesse was right. It was a hot air balloon in a harlequin pattern of blue and green, the school colors.

Ragged cheering broke out in the stands.

"It must say something like 'Go, West Mount,' " Susan said.

"Wait a minute," Jesse said. "It's coming our way. Maybe we'll be able to read it."

Michael's grip on Ann Lee's arm suddenly tightened. "Ouch!" she cried. "Michael, what's wrong?" She looked at him in alarm.

"That balloon! Look at it!" He licked his lips nervously.

"Isn't it cute!" Ann Lee exclaimed. "Somebody's made a balloon in the school colors!"

"It's going against the wind," Michael observed in a tense voice.

Jesse edged nearer to hear what Michael was saying. "So what? What does that mean?"

"It looks to me like somebody's telling that sucker just where to go. It's radio-controlled. It wouldn't go against the wind unless it was powered somehow. I read about a stunt like that once. Some guys at this hotshot technical school got one fixed to explode all over the opposing team. When it exploded, it turned out to be full of baby powder."

"But this one's not going toward the other team's side." Jesse pointed out. "It's coming out here toward us!"

Ann Lee tugged at Michael's coat. "What are you getting at, Michael?" she asked. "Explain it to me."

He looked at her a moment, hesitating. "I told C.G. about the balloon stunt those college guys pulled. It seems the balloon was guided by radio. C.G. said the radio probably controlled the jets of air that helped propel the thing. It works sort of on the same principle as a hair dryer. This looks like the same thing to me."

"And now—our new homecoming queen," the loudspeaker boomed. "Miss Ann Lee Smith!"

Ann Lee gasped. Shrieks sounded around her as the other girls clapped and feigned mad delight. Susan clapped and shrieked with the rest of them, but her blusher stood out in spots on the whiteness of her shocked face.

Jesse put his arm around Susan's waist. "Forget it," he said quietly. "It doesn't matter. I know how you feel. I hate to lose, too, but you're still the best." He gave her a little squeeze.

"This stupid homecoming junk doesn't change who you are, you know." He lifted his gaze to stare at the balloon.

Somewhere inside, Susan knew that Jesse's words made sense, but she couldn't seem to take them in at the moment. She had to summon every ounce of her strength to force her stiff lips into a smile. The only thing that mattered to her now was that she keep from disgracing herself. In her crushing defeat, it was absolutely essential that she look like a good sport.

Michael pushed Ann Lee forward to accept the crown, but all the while he kept watching the slow-moving balloon. It seemed to be emitting a hum. He thought he heard it for a second and then decided it must be his imagination.

The Student Council president, Jimmy Cooper, strode toward Ann Lee. The crown glittered in his hands as he lifted it over her head.

Tears stung Susan's eyes. All those years that she had been friendly to everyone, even when she hadn't felt like it! It hadn't been enough. The kids didn't like her enough, after all.

She knew she would have to look away, past Ann Lee and the crown if she was going to keep from sobbing aloud. She focused on the green- and blue-patterned balloon. It looked blurry through her tears and somehow bigger than it had before. She blinked her tears away rapidly. It was getting closer! That was what was happening! From where she stood, Ann Lee's dark head and the gilt crown were silhouetted against the bottom of the balloon. It was low and coming very slowly toward them. It seemed to loom behind Jimmy like some ill-defined menace.

She grasped Jesse's lapel. "Do something, Jesse!"

"What?" Jesse's eyes shifted quickly from Susan to Ann Lee and back again.

"The balloon," Susan cried. "Can't you see it's headed right for Ann Lee! It could have a bomb in it or—or anything. We've got to stop it."

Jesse stared unblinkingly at the balloon. "You really think there's a bomb in the thing?"

"Or something bad." Susan twisted a strand of hair around her finger. She gazed at the balloon like a person hypnotized. "Jesse, you know what C.G. is like! You heard what Michael said. She's behind this. We've got to *do* something. Can't you do *anything?*"

She had not bothered to lower her voice. Ann Lee cast an anxious glance over her shoulder. Jimmy, too, shot her a nervous look.

Jesse tried to gauge the distance to the balloon. It looked to him as if it was made out of something like varnished tissue paper. It was, at least, some kind of very thin, light stuff because he had seen that it folded some and wrinkled as it moved across the field. He could see the fluidity of the air inside it. He judged that it just might be possible to put a tear in it.

"Okay," he said at last. "I guess I'd better try to bring it down."

"What's going on?" cried Keesha.

In a sudden blast of sound behind them, the band began playing the alma mater. The noise bored into Susan's head until she wanted to cover her ears and scream. She wished the band would shut up so she could think.

"What do you have that I could throw at it?" Jesse asked her. "It needs to be something pretty heavy—something sharp would even be better. I'm not sure this is going to work, Susan." He patted his pockets.

She could have told him his suit pockets weren't going to yield a Swiss army knife. She gritted her teeth. If only she could *think*.

The student body president looked behind him uneasily and blanched. He managed to keep holding the crown over Ann Lee's head, but his hands shook.

Improvise! a voice inside Susan reminded her. Rainey had said it was always possible to improvise. Suddenly Susan bent over and slipped off one shoe. Recklessly, she put the high heel in her mouth and popped off its rubber tip. This maneuver exposed the metal spike that was the core of the heel. One part of her mind saw a headline in the school paper: "Member of Homecoming Court Eats Shoe." But throwing the shoe just might work. The rubber tip was gritty with dirt, and she spit distastefully as she placed the shoe in Jesse's hand.

He took it without looking down at it. His eyes were on the balloon. Susan started to warn him not to hit Ann Lee or Jimmy, but then bit her tongue. She was afraid of ruining his concentration.

Shifting his balance, Jesse threw with all his strength.

Susan didn't see the shoe flying through the air, but she saw the balloon dimple deeply when it was hit. She watched, scarcely breathing. The balloon seemed to sag a bit. Had the shoe actually opened a tear?

Next, a softness showed in the balloon, a slight crumpling and wilting. It started to lose altitude. All at once the air rushed out of it, and it plummeted to the ground. It lay on the field deflated, but still recognizable as a balloon.

Pop! A bang like that of a cherry bomb went off and they all jumped. Susan glanced down and saw that her hands were trembling. She could make out a bulge under the balloon, which she decided was its basket. Something white and powdery stained the turf around it.

Ann Lee blinked in bewilderment. Jimmy had dropped the crown on her head precipitously when the explosion went off, and she was forced to steady it with her hand.

"It's okay." Michael spoke with his teeth clenched into a smile. "Wave to the people, and then we're off."

"Did C.G. do that?" Ann Lee gasped.

"Who else?"

Ann Lee refused to look down at the deflated balloon. Smiling, she waved to the crowd. Michael took her arm and they turned to lead the procession off the field. Ann Lee's shoulders were rigid. She felt as if a sniper had his sights trained on her back. The fifty yards they had to traverse seemed more like a mile. She was besieged by a totally irrational fear that C.G. was running after her, and she yearned above all to feel the comforting weight of a hockey stick in her hands.

When they at last reached the locker room, Ann Lee sagged against the building, trying to catch her breath. She was surprised to see that Mona and Keesha and their dates were trailing back to the stands to watch the rest of the game. Football players were jogging back onto the field, and she could hear the welcoming cheers from the stands. Her eyes met Michael's. No one but they themselves seemed to realize that the homecoming court had had a narrow escape.

"Let's get out of here," Michael said.

"You mean, leave before the game is over?"

"I don't know about you, but I have *had* it."

Over by the door to the locker room, Susan was leaning with her head against Jesse's chest, her shoulders heaving.

Michael jerked his head toward her. "And I'm not the only one who's had it." He turned. "Say, Jesse," he called. "You two want to get pizza?"

Jesse touched Susan's shoulder and raised his eyebrows questioningly.

She wiped her sleeve across her eyes and nodded. "All this excitement," she gasped. "I guess I'm just coming unglued. If I can just go somewhere warm and get something to drink I'll be okay."

Herbie Cantrell, the team manager, brushed past Michael to go into the locker room.

"Hey, Susan," said Michael. "Isn't that your shoe?"

Herbie held up a small black pump. "This yours? Had to get it off the field before play began."

Susan limped over and took it from him. "Thank you, Herbie." She managed a feeble smile.

"What happened to the balloon?" Michael asked.

Herbie shrugged. "Dunno. Some guy came out and got it."

"Some 'guy' in a black leather jacket, I'll bet," Susan sniffed.

They could hear the cheerleaders going crazy as the football players charged. But they didn't bother to look out on the field.

"I don't know about the rest of you," Michael said flatly. "But I am out of this place."

"Where are you parked?" asked Jesse.

Ann Lee recognized that the decision to leave had already been made without her. She was not exactly sorry. She admitted to herself that it would be wonderful to get out of the cold and collapse somewhere. She just hoped it didn't come out publicly that the homecoming queen had cut out of the game at halftime.

Homecoming queen! Her title still had a strangeness to it. Glancing at Susan, she felt almost like an impostor, not like a genuine homecoming queen. But still she felt a certain satisfaction when she took off the gilt crown and slipped it over her wrist.

They walked toward the parking area behind the stadium, hearing the roar of the crowd behind them. Someone had scored.

"You're a blinking hero," Michael told Jesse feelingly. "Another three minutes and we would have been coughing up baby powder. Jeez, what a close call that was!"

"I knew Jesse wouldn't miss," Susan said.

"I'd be in pretty bad shape if I couldn't hit a target that big. Of course," Jesse added, "I'm not exactly used to pitching a shoe."

Luckily, their cars hadn't been blocked in by others in the parking area. They were able to maneuver their way out and drive on to the Pizza Hut.

Ann Lee and Michael arrived first. They stood under the light at the entrance, waiting. Ann Lee's face puckered anxiously when Susan and Jesse got out of the Camaro. As they walked up the sidewalk, Susan's left shoe made a metallic click on the pavement with her every step, and Ann Lee was suddenly glad she had put her crown out of sight in Michael's glove compartment. "Your poor shoe!" Ann Lee cried. "Do you think it's ruined? Can you get it fixed?"

Susan shrugged. "Don't worry about my shoe. It doesn't matter."

"I don't know what I would have done if that balloon had exploded over my head." Ann Lee was seized by a sudden shiver. "Honestly, you saved my life!" She knew she was being Susan's admiring chorus again, but this time she didn't care.

The four friends stepped together into the warmth of the restaurant. Behind a brightly lit counter at the front, a boy with a bad complexion was briskly painting a round slab of pizza dough with tomato sauce. The spicy smells of pizza were borne toward Susan from the big ovens, and her stomach growled with hunger. She realized with mild surprise that she didn't feel as miserable as she would have expected, given the circumstances. After all, she did have the satisfaction of having behaved pretty well. Maybe it was true, as her mother was always saying, that winning or losing was not all that mattered.

She peered into the gloom of the dining area. In the corner were the glowing pastel tubes of the jukebox, and the steady throb of a rock beat sounded in the room. Beyond, she saw points of red light made by small flickering candles placed in red glasses on each table.

"Blake!" Michael whooped suddenly. "Hey there, you turkey. How'd you get here?"

Susan's eyes adjusted to the darkness and she made out Blake and Rainey huddled over one of the flickering red candles in a corner booth.

Michael charged over to their booth, and the rest of them trailed after him. Only two slices of pizza remained on Blake and Rainey's metal serving plate.

"So you two decided to cut out early, too, huh?" Michael looked first at Blake and then at Rainey.

Their eyes met his sheepishly.

"Well, did you even stay to see the halftime show?" demanded Michael.

Blake slipped down a little in his seat. "Naturally, we wanted to see the presentation of the homecoming court and see who won and all that," he began.

"We left about halftime actually," Rainey put in. "We—" She looked helplessly at Blake.

"Had some things we wanted to talk about," Blake finished triumphantly.

Susan saw that they had worked out the last of their differences. They looked so pleased with themselves and each other that they practically begged to be tied up in pink ribbon. What did they know of cold journeys over the football field, of exploding balloons and the bitterness of defeat? She supposed she felt the way battle veterans felt when they got home and saw everybody still hanging out at the mall.

"Then you don't even know who got homecoming queen?" Michael said incredulously. "It was our own Ann Lee!" He held Ann Lee's hand up in the gesture of a victorious champion.

The look of stark surprise on Blake's face was balm for Susan's wounded spirit. She would survive, she reminded herself—she was strong. And didn't she recall reading that Cybill Shepherd had only been runner-up for the Junior Miss title? Nobody had ever even heard of the girl who won. That just goes to show you, she thought.

Everyone began talking at once, trying to explain to Blake and Rainey what had happened.

"Baby powder?" Blake kept saying. "Why baby powder? I don't get it."

"It was supposed to explode all over us," said Michael. "We were supposed to stand there with our faces white, trying to get baby powder off our good clothes and looking like idiots."

"The idea was to humiliate us," Ann Lee said.

The sound of a motorcycle outside the window cast them all into sudden silence. They looked at one another with wide eyes. Ann Lee slid swiftly into the next booth and pressed her nose against the window. "I can't see a thing," she reported. "Can you see anything, Rainey?"

Rainey peered through the glass. "Not a thing."

Suddenly the door of the restaurant was pushed open with such force that the paper napkin beside Rainey's plate fluttered. Their heads snapped around as if attached to the same marionette string.

A boy in black leather sauntered in, his thumbs hooked on the belt loops of his jeans. His hair was swept back into a flip of curls behind his ears. He had full, deeply curved lips that appeared to be curled into a permanent sneer, and he surveyed the room with open contempt. Right behind him, clad in gleaming black leather, was C.G.

"Jeez, it's Craig Ousterhout," murmured Michael.

"And C.G." Ann Lee's voice quavered.

At first they could make out little more of C.G. than her silhouette, but when she moved over to the other side of Craig, the red exit sign near the ladies' room shone on her face, momentarily making her look like a motorcycle rider from hell. She turned slowly, surveying the room. Then she said something to Craig. Looking straight at their group, she favored them with a slow smile. They were too taken aback to respond. She gazed at them a second, looking faintly amused, then nodded graciously and took a seat next to Craig.

Ann Lee realized that her mouth was hanging open and she abruptly snapped it shut.

Michael finally pulled himself together enough to lift his hand in greeting. "Change places with me, Blake," he muttered under his breath. "So I don't have to sit and look at her all night."

Jesse and Susan slid out of the booth so that Blake and Michael could change seats. "What does it mean?" Ann Lee asked anxiously. "What do you think, Rainey? Would you say that was a friendly smile?"

Michael sighed and slumped down in his seat. "I think it was."

There was a long silence.

"Tie him down, Ann Lee," Blake teased. "This could be a serious setback. We're going to have to stand watch to keep him from doing something rash."

"Very funny!" Michael glared at him. "I just don't happen to think that's funny, Farraby, if you don't mind."

"Sorry."

"Some people can actually entertain two contradictory ideas at one time. It's kind of like being able to walk and chew gum at once. Have you heard of that? I can sort of see some of C.G.'s good qualities while at the same time fervently praying that our paths never cross again. Do you follow me?"

"I follow you," Ann Lee said in a small voice.

"Good." He patted her hand. "Because you're the only one I'm worried about."

Ann Lee's face glowed—homecoming queen, and Michael actually liked her!

"So this means C.G. is finished being mad?" Susan asked.

"I think so," Michael said. "That's my considered opinion. My guess is that she had her fun and now she's got other fish to fry. Craig Ousterhout, for example."

Ann Lee was still anxious. "You think this means peace, really?"

Michael shrugged.

Rainey cupped her chin in her hand. Her voice was dreamy. "Yeah, peace and love and happiness ever after."

Michael looked at her indignantly. "Good grief, Rainey. What are you on!"

Blake's eyes met Rainey's and they fell into helpless laughter.

"Stop it," Ann Lee whispered anxiously. "What if she thinks we're laughing at her? You guys! Stop it!"

"I can't help it," Rainey wiped tears from her eyes.

"It's okay." Blake grabbed Rainey's hands. "We can stop." But his eyes crinkled at the corners and his grin was broad and sort of stupid looking.

"You two have gone nuts," Michael said flatly.

"I know it," Rainey said. "But I'm not laughing anymore. Look! I'm very serious." She held her napkin up in front of her face, and when she took it away, her features were arranged in an expression of suitable gravity. But inside her the happy laughter went on and on.

About the Author

JANICE HARRELL decided she wanted to be a writer
when she was in the fourth grade. She grew up in
Florida and received her master's and doctorate de-
grees in eighteenth-century English literature from the
University of Florida. After teaching college English
for a number of years, she began to write full time.

She lives in Rocky Mount, North Carolina, with her
husband, a psychologist, and their daughter. Ms. Harrell is a compulsive traveler—some of the countries
she has visited are Greece, France, Egypt, Italy, England, and Spain—and she loves taking photographs.